A MEMORY
and other stories

By the same author

Novels

THE HOUSE IN CLEWE STREET
MARY O'GRADY

Short Stories

TALES FROM BECTIVE BRIDGE
THE LONG AGO
THE BECKER WIVES
THE LIKELY STORY
A SINGLE LADY
THE PATRIOT SON
SELECTED STORIES
THE GREAT WAVE
THE STORIES OF MARY LAVIN
(Collected edition selected from the stories above)
IN THE MIDDLE OF THE FIELDS
HAPPINESS

A MEMORY
and other stories
by Mary Lavin

CONSTABLE
LONDON

First published in Great Britain 1972
by Constable and Company Ltd
10 Orange Street, London WC2H 7EG
Copyright © 1972 Mary Lavin
ISBN 0 09 458770 1

In this collection 'Trastevere' first appeared
in *The New Yorker*

Printed in Great Britain by The Anchor Press Ltd,
and bound by Wm. Brendon & Son Ltd,
both of Tiptree, Essex

For my son-in-law
Desmond MacMahon

Contents

Tomb of an Ancestor

It was the hour of the siesta – in a small damp town in the west of Ireland. There, although at times the sun shone, it shone only in the glittering early hours. By noon it was gone, unlikely to shine again till evening. Then it lit the whole sky with a forlorn light.

The town was once encircled by a rampart. This in part was fallen, but deep in the town's core was an inner wall, intact except for one gap. Inside this again was the ruin of an old friary and an ancient burial ground long closed to funerals. Of the friary nothing remained but a single lancet window held up like the eye of a needle to be threaded with light. The surrounding tombs and graves were smothered with weeds and the wall itself was weighted with masses of ivy which, when it could find no further foothold on the stone, reared into the air, flowering and fruiting wildly. From a distance the outline of this ivy against the sky might be taken for an extravagant cloud formation presaging storm. In fact its heavy masses overhanging the streets gave shelter from the rain, and on wet days the country people when they came into town to do their shopping were glad to tie up their ponies and traps under these great canopies.

The town was once prosperous. The older premises – tall edifices of cut-stone, with rambling yards and

9

out-offices – were more like the residences of landed squires than small town shopkeepers. These magnificent old properties still gave standing to their occupants, even in cases where, like Duffys, the occupants had fallen on lean times. Duffys stock often went so low they had nothing to display in their windows but dummy cartons and a large gilded replica of a whisky bottle. The lettering on the Duffy showboard was so faded, their shop was sometimes mistaken for a warehouse belonging to the Dermodys' thriving business on the opposite side of the street. Small as the town was, the same names were often repeated from shopfront to shopfront, but if a blood tie had ever existed between the occupants, it had long been erased from memory by the friction of daily dealings. When men and women have to live at close quarters, the pull of blood may have to be let weaken in order that life may have its proper diversity.

And although, like the people, the granite blocks of the houses must have come from a common quarry, they too now were diversified by weathering and wear.

Duffys, close under the friary walls, was covered with a livid green lichen, whereas Dermodys across the street glowed russet and red. But high up, near the roofs, all the houses sprouted strangely delicate blossoms that raised themselves upwards on thin pinlike stems, and trembled like antennae feeling for – well, for what? It could hardly have been for sunlight, although weeds grew freely everywhere, and in strange places here and there trees, seeded by chance, had managed to spring into spindly growth. Strange to say, in these trees even on dull and rainy days small birds sang – having no doubt learned that if they did not sing in the rain they might seldom sing at all.

So, with birds singing, and yellow weeds abounding, there was often a feeling of summer in the air. And here too, just as in the scorching streets of Cordoba, at the noon-day hour, human activity ground to a halt, and the adult population submitted to a curfew of lethargy. Only a few took to their beds – an obese publican, perhaps, or a pregnant woman – the others became inert in the posture in which the hour found them. It was as if the hour itself was sleep, or even death, that had caught them unawares, flowing over them like lava, fixing them fast. Here, a woman at a kitchen table stared into a cup of cold tea. There, an old man leaned his weight on the handle of a yard-brush, and drowsed on his feet. And everywhere aged cats and dogs lay flattened across doorways, or stretched themselves out in the dust of the street. A few young dogs sometimes evaded the general inertia, and in a pack headed off out of the town for the green fields to worry ewes and suck eggs. At this hour too the children roved in packs, but they rarely ventured far beyond the ramparts. They were not at ease in the open country. And although from their back windows all their lives they had seen the green fields flashing between the tin roofs of shed and privy, there was only one field outside the town in which they felt really safe. This was the New Cemetery.

In this large and treeless field, bright, open, and kept free of weeds, they ran about freely. Where safer could they be than in God's acre?

There were not many graves in the New Cemetery, and these were mostly huddled together near the entrance gate. Not that the children hesitated to step on a grave. Wasn't it their own dead that lay below? Their own family names that were carved on the headstones? Hardly a child but had a relative buried here, if only a still-born baby, an infant sister, or brother. As for Molly Higgins – both her father and her mother were buried here, although they died soon after Molly was born up in Dublin and where they would have been put down in a Paupers' Plot if Molly's uncle had not had them brought back at his own expense to their native town. Indeed, Molly herself would have been put into an orphanage if the same uncle had not taken her and reared her up with Mickser.

In the bright open spaces of the New Cemetery the children felt much the same solidarity they felt with their own shadows, also prone and silent, while they ran about overhead splitting the air with their shouts.

And before they started to play, when the children were picking sides, Mickser Dermody and Jamesey Duffy, the two leaders, always stood each on his own family mound, and the others, in turn as they were picked, sat down, each on the grave proper to his side.

Picking sides was a mere formality. The sides were always the same. Mickser always picked Ned Conroy, Tim Hynes and his own cousin Molly. Jamesey always picked his sister Annie, Tommy Mack and Matt Foley. Only the Morrisroes – being identical twins – were interchangeable, and if someone was missing, they were lumped together as one. At other times when a twin was picked, the other, without being told, hopped over to the other side, both beaming happily as if in those moments they were given a vestige more identity than had been given them by their begetters. Then, ready to play, the two sides would stand up.

But what would they play? What but the old, old game that the children of men have played since time began, each in the idiom of his day: Dux et Imperator in the time of Suetonius, Christians and Infidels during the Crusades, Cathies and Proddies at the Reformation. And always, behind it, was the same principle of You against Me – since the game was first played outside the Garden of Eden with only two children to play it – Cain and Abel.

One sultry afternoon in mid-July, the children had assembled on the steps of the Market Cross, and were about to set off for the cemetery when they saw that Mickser wasn't with them. They looked at Molly. She had never before come out to play without him.

'My Uncle called him back,' Molly said, with a worried look.

But next minute Mickser came galloping up the street, slapping his thigh as he ran and uttering triumphant yells.

'Yippee – yippee, I'm going away! To school! To boarding school,' he yelled, and producing a sepia coloured postcard from his hip pocket he passed it around. 'It's a castle. Look! There's a moat with real water in it. And a drawbridge – a sort of one – I mean – because it has to be left open most of the time so parents can get in to visit. But I'll tell you something else!' He lowered his voice. 'There's a room in it that had to be blocked up, windows and all, because it's *haunted*!'

'Oh Mickser!' His own followers forgot their impending loss in the first flush of their pride in him. And even the Duffys for a moment felt only curiosity.

'Show me!' Tommy Mack cried as he grabbed the postcard from Ned Conroy, and Annie Duffy and Matt Foley were peering over his shoulder. Molly had apparently seen it before. Jamesey alone made no effort to see the card. Shoving his hands into his pockets he was staring down at his feet and frowning.

'When are you going, Mickser?' Molly asked.

'September, I suppose,' Mickser said, offhandedly.

Molly brightened. 'Oh, that's ages away,' she said. 'They might change their minds before then!'

Mickser stared at her in amazement. 'No fear! I won't let them, I want to go,' he said. But when he saw the watery smile she gave him he felt badly. 'Don't worry, Molly. My father and mother will be hiring a car and coming up to see me fairly often – and they'll be bringing you. I'll show you round,' he said proudly.

But at this Jamesey gave a loud guffaw.

'That's a good one,' he sneered. 'As if they'll let a girl into a boys' school!'

Mickser swung around. 'She's my cousin, isn't she?'

'What difference does that make? She's a girl, isn't she?'

'Oh, don't mind him, Mickser,' Molly said. 'He's just jealous because his father is too mean to send him.'

Immediately Annie Duffy rushed to her father's defence.

'Say that again, Molly Higgins!' she challenged.

But at that moment the summer air was rent with a shriek.

Instantly the Morrisroes, who had got hold of the postcard and were poring over it let it fall from their fingers as they groped for each other's hands and stared at the old friary from which the cry had come.

'What is it?' they whispered, terrified.

'Oh, it's only an old bird,' Mickser said irritably, 'or a badger, or something.'

But then the cry came again. Bird or beast, the cry made them all draw closer, and the Morrisroes' teeth began to chatter.

'It's only a bird I tell you,' Mickser repeated. 'Come on. What are we going to play?'

But Jamesey's eyes had narrowed.

'How do you know it's a bird, Mickser Dermody? I heard an old man in our shop one night telling my father about a woman that was buried in the friary with all her rings on her fingers, and robbers heard about it, and stole into the graveyard one night and dug up her coffin!'

'Oh Jamesey!' They all shuddered.

'Ssh. Let him go on,' Mickser said.

'Well,' Jamesey dropped his voice to a sepulchral note, 'when they dug up the coffin and broke it open, they couldn't get the rings off her because when you die you get all swelled up. They had to saw off her fingers.'

'*Saw* them off?' There was a general gasp. 'Oh Jamesey!'

But Mickser's lip curled with contempt.

'And will you tell me *where*,' he demanded, '*where* did they find a saw so handy? *In a graveyard*? In the *middle of the night*?'

There was a titter from the Morrisroes, but Jamesey silenced them with a look.

'Are you calling me a liar, Mickser Dermody?' he demanded.

'No,' said Mickser slowly and levelly. 'Not if you can prove it.'

It was a dare! Jamesey stared around him like one caught in his own trap. It was Mickser's turn now to put his hands in his pockets. 'All you've got to do,' he said magnanimously, 'is get a spade and dig down a little way into the ground, because the coffin will be rotted away. You'll come on the skeleton in a minute. You won't have to wait till the middle of the night either like the robbers, because nobody ever goes into the old friary now, even in daylight. Once you're over the wall no one will see you. Or hear you! No one will know you're there at all.' Carried away by his magnanimity, he laid his arm across Jamesey's shoulders. 'You don't have to bring back the *whole* skeleton – only the hand. And if it has no fingers on it, well, then we might believe you.'

The children turned and stared in the direction of the lonely ruin hidden behind its high wall, with the massive weight of ivy.

But Mickser read their minds.

'You'll only have to bring back the hand,' he repeated. 'The whole thing will fall apart when you touch it. It's only in pictures and museums skeletons are in one piece because the bones are strung together on wire. When you first dig them up they're all in pieces. You can pick up any bit you want, a skull, or a shin-bone; any part at all.' In the awed silence that followed this information, Mickser turned away. 'Don't worry,' he told his followers. 'He won't do it,' he said. 'He'd be too scared!'

'Scared? Is it me?' Jamesey looked outraged. 'Well, that's a good one! And my father is the only Patriot in this town – the only man who was up in Dublin and took part in the Easter Rising. And *wounded* into the bargain! Got by a sniper he was – in O'Connell Street. Or hit by shrapnel! The doctors couldn't rightly tell which.'

'Oh Jamesey!' Molly's gentle face clouded. 'Was that how your father got his limp?'

Mickser only laughed. 'Bah!' he said. 'Doesn't everyone know it was going to Fairyhouse Races old Duffy was that day. He was only up in O'Connell Street trying to cadge a free lift out to the racetrack when the shooting started. He may have been hit alright, hit by accident!' As there was another snigger from the Morrisroes, Mickser was emboldened to a further taunt. 'A hole in the toe of his boot was what I'd say he got,' he said, and at the good of his own joke he himself laughed long and loudly.

Jamesey's face that had gone red, now went black with rage.

'That's a dirty lie. Who told you that, Mickser Dermody?'

'My mother told me,' Mickser said piously.

'Your *mother*?' Jamesey gave a short, contemptuous laugh. 'And what would *your* mother know about the Rising? Where was *she*, I'd like to know, when men like my father were out fighting for their country? I'll tell you! Behind the counter of your rotten old shop, bowing and scraping to the British Constabulary, and sucking up to them for fear she'd lose their custom. I bet she didn't know there was a Rising until it was over. And then she started sucking up to the Free Staters.'

There was another snigger at this, but Mickser

B

wasn't so sure now that it came from the Morrisroes:
it came from somewhere behind Jamesey.

'What's wrong with making money anyway?' he
asked, a bit taken aback. 'If you Duffys paid more
heed to the till you wouldn't be the way you are now,
with your father without a penny to send you to boarding school. You Duffys are too busy running down to
the chapel every minute, craw-thumping and lighting
candles. You're half-cracked with piousity.' He turned
to the others. 'You can't deny his Aunt Sara is half-
cracked, can you? Don't forget the day she drove us
in front of her with her umbrella all the way back
to the New Cemetery, and made us empty our
pockets and put back the jackstones we'd been all day
selecting.'

Would any of them ever forget that day? The New
Cemetery was the only place a decent set of pebbles
could be got – smooth and evenly matched, and every
Spring they went out there to get a new set for the
coming season until the day Miss Sara Duffy came on
them. Mickser mimicked the old maid's voice.

'*It's a grave sin, children. You must put them back at
once.*' And as he mimicked her he made a motion of
poking Molly in the back with the point of an imaginary umbrella.

But one of the Morrisroes nudged the other who
plucked Molly by the sleeve.

'What sin was it, Molly?'

Molly gave them a scathing glance. 'It was no sin at
all! Didn't you hear Mickser say Sara Duffy is cracked.'

Mickser tapped his own forehead. 'She's got *scruples*.
That's what's wrong with her.'

Scruples? Was that a disease?

'It's a sort of a disease,' Mickser explained. 'They think everything is a sin. They don't get put in the asylum, because they're sort of harmless, but everyone knows they're cuckoo all the same! Were you never in the same pew with Sara Duffy on a Saturday night going to Confession? When the priest gives her absolution and closes the shutter, do you think she comes out? Oh no. Not Sara Duffy! She stays inside, trying to think up more sins. And when the priest opens the shutter again she's still there! One Saturday night when the Canon opened the slide for the third time and found her still inside he slammed it shut in her face. Like this.' Mickser brought the flat of his hands together with a clack. 'And when he found her still inside the fourth time, and the fifth time, the shutter was opening and closing so fast – click-clack click-clack – you'd swear it was butter clappers at work. And at last he gave out a roar and took off his stole and jumped out of the box, and dragged her into the aisle. "Come out of that, you foolish woman," he yelled, "and stop wasting my time. Can't you see the chapel is full of good, honest to God sinners with decent sins to tell!" Oh, it was a right laugh.'

To hear Mickser tell it certainly was a laugh. Even Tommy Mack sniggered. But Jamesey was waiting for the laughing to stop.

'You think you're very smart, don't you, Mickser Dermody? Well, let me tell you it's better to have too much religion than to have none at all. Doesn't everyone know your mother used to put you and Molly in the same tub when Molly first came to live with you. And that's – '

'Oh-oh-*oh*. That's a terrible sin,' Annie Duffy and

Tommy Mack said both together, and one of the Morrisroes who was standing near Mickser hopped back nervously from him.

For the first time Mickser was really taken aback. 'That's not true, Molly. Is it?' he said.

Molly didn't answer, but her cheeks were blazing. 'If it was a sin, what sin was it, Jamesey Duffy?' she cried. And turning to Annie Duffy she repeated the question, because all the girls were better than the boys at catechism.

'Maybe it was simony,' Annie said. She wasn't sure what simony was, but it had an ugly sound. The others all looked uneasily at Molly.

Molly tossed her head. 'Simony is stealing from God. That's what simony is!'

Again one of the Morrisroes nudged the other. 'Is that why Miss Duffy made us put back the jackstones?'

'Not at all,' Molly scoffed. 'That was only sacrilege. It wouldn't be simony unless we sold them.'

The Morrisroes conferred again quickly.

'Swapping isn't selling, is it?'

No one paid them any heed. They were all racking their brains trying to think of special sins.

'Perhaps it's a Reserved Sin,' Molly herself suggested, because after the first shame she was beginning to feel a certain sense of importance, and a reserved sin was one for which absolution could not be got from a priest. You'd have to be sent to a Bishop!

A gleam of malice came in Annie Duffy's eyes. 'Maybe it's The Sin against the Holy Ghost. There's no absolution for *that* at all, not *even* from a bishop, because you don't know you've committed it till you're dead, and then it's too *late*!'

But Mickser had had enough. 'Don't mind her, Molly, didn't I tell you the Duffys are cuckoo. They never think about anything only sin and damnation.'

'Better to think about them now than when it's too late,' Jamesey said darkly. 'Not like you lot. My mother said hell wasn't good enough for you Dermodys after what your grandfather did to Molly's mother and father.'

'Oh Jamesey!' Even his sister Annie seemed to think this was going too far. But surprisingly Molly turned to Mickser.

'He *was* a mean old man,' she said. 'But he couldn't stop them loving each other! Nobody can kill love!'

Except for Jamesey, sudden smiles broke over every face. They all knew the story of Molly's parents. Annie even ran over and threw her arm around Molly.

'Nobody can stop people *loving* each other. Nothing can kill true love!'

Love! With what relief the children heard that word after all the talk of sin and corruption. It was as if the pavement under their feet had cracked and a blossom-tree had forced itself upwards and shaken its fragrance over them.

'They eloped, didn't they, Molly?' she asked, smiling rapturously, because she already knew the story.

But Jamesey was scowling at his sister. 'I don't see what's so great about eloping,' he said.

'Oh, shut up, Jamesey,' Annie said. 'It's so romantic.'

'I will not shut up,' said Jamesey. 'Eloping is the same as getting married, only it's doing the thing on the cheap. It's when people are *crossed in love* or die of a broken heart that it's romantic.' He gave Annie an impatient push. 'Like our cousin Ada! That was someone romantic for you!' When Annie looked puzzled Jamesey shook her with exasperation. 'The one our mother is always going on about! The one the locket belonged to – the locket in our mother's work-box – '

'Oh, her!' Annie *did* remember. 'Our great-aunt Ada?'

'She was some relation anyway,' Jamesey said, less certainly. He was regretting he hadn't listened more attentively when his mother was telling them about her. 'I know one thing!' he said proudly. 'She was the most beautiful girl that ever walked the streets of this town!' Yes, Annie remembered hearing that, she could vouch for the truth of that and she remembered something else. 'People held their breath when she passed them in the street!'

'Why did they hold their breath, Annie?' Molly was looking as rapturously at her as she had looked at Molly a few minutes earlier.

'I suppose it was because she was so gentle,' Annie said. 'When she walked across a room you wouldn't hear her unless a board creaked!'

Molly looked down at the strong boots on her feet, if Ada was so light and airy her slippers must have been as soft as gloves. 'She must have been a real beauty,' she sighed.

'She *was*,' Jamesey cried. 'And she died of a broken heart. *That's* something to boast about.'

But Mickser was looking suspiciously at him.

'How is it you never told us about this before?'

'Hush, Mickser!' Molly said softly. 'Tell us more, Jamesey.'

Jamesey frowned, as he threshed around in his mind for something else to tell about his romantic ancestor, but he could remember nothing more.

Annie could though. 'Do you remember what she said when she was dying, Jamesey!' she cried. 'Tell them that.'

'Oh *that*?' Jamesey got so excited he could hardly tell it coherently. 'Her last words when she was dying?' He threw out his hand dramatically. 'She was lying on a couch downstairs with the family all around her (the doctor wouldn't let them move her upstairs she was so weak). And she was dying –' Here Jamesey was so carried away that he threw back his own head and closed his eyes. 'They thought she was dead,' he whispered, 'but when she opened her eyes again do you know what she said? –' His own voice was now so feeble and laboured, they all had to move closer to hear him. '*Did the cat – get – her milk*?' he whispered in a dying cadence.

'Those weren't her *very last words, Jamesey*?' Molly's incredulity was voiced so loudly Jamesey's eyes flew open.

To his astonishment Molly was trying not to laugh and one of the Morrisroes not able to smother his laughter gave a snort. As for Mickser, Mickser was so amused he threw himself down on the ground, and did a back-somersault as he imitated the dying girl!

'Did – the – ould cat – get her milk?' he croaked. 'Did – the – ould cat – get – her milk?'

The spell of love was broken. They all began to jump up and down, chanting garbled versions of the dying Ada's words.

'*Did yez give the old cat its milk*? Did yez ... ?'

Molly was the first to stop laughing. Overcome by remorse, she put her hand on Jamesey's arm. 'Don't mind them, Jamesey,' she said gently. 'It was very nice of her to think of the cat.' But she still looked puzzled. 'Wasn't it a wonder it wasn't *him* she was thinking about, and not an old cat?'

Mickser sat up. 'That's right. Who was he anyway? You didn't tell us. He couldn't have been much, who-ever he was, if he jilted her.'

Furiously Jamesey turned on him. 'Who said she was jilted?'

'Well, if she wasn't jilted, why didn't she marry him?'

Yes, why didn't she? They all looked to Jamesey for an answer to this.

'Maybe she wouldn't be *let* marry him,' Jamesey hazarded.

Not satisfied Molly tossed her head. 'I'd like to see anyone try to stop *me* if I was her!' But she did not want to be unkind to the dead lovers. 'Maybe one of them was delicate?' she suggested.

Mickser was never one for small niceties like that.

'Who was the man?' he demanded. Perhaps Ada, for all her beauty, was only one more old maid like so many, whose lover was a dream-lover? 'Maybe she was in love with the old tom-cat,' he cried and over-come by this witticism, he threw himself down again and did another back-somersault.

Almost in despair Jamesey shook Annie's arm. 'Wasn't there a name on that locket?' he cried.

'No,' said Annie. 'Not a name, only an initial.' Then suddenly she remembered something else. 'But it was written in hair,' she cried. 'Jet black hair! It must have been *his* hair!'

A fat lot of use that was, Jamesey seemed to say, but he knew he had to make the best of it.

'See!' he cried. 'There you are!'

Mickser sat up.

'What initial was it?' he insisted.

James and Annie looked at each other. They couldn't remember.

'I think it was a "V",' Annie ventured at last.

'There you are!' Jamesey said again. 'It was V.'

But the heart of the mystery still remained. V for what?

'Oh, try to remember, Annie,' the Morrisroes pleaded.

Once more the threat of being called liars hung over the Duffys, when suddenly Molly's voice rang out.

'*V was for Vinny.*'

'Molly? How do *you* know?' Mickser stared at her in amazement.

'Because we have a locket too,' she cried. 'Your mother showed it to me once. It's gold, and it's in the shape of a heart. And inside there's an initial. And that initial is written with hair *too* – beautiful golden hair!'

'But what has that got to do with the Duffys' locket?' Mickser asked, flustered.

'It belonged to our great-uncle Vinny,' Molly said, 'and the initial inside was "A". Oh, don't you see, Mickser? It must have been *her* hair – Ada's.'

Suddenly Jamesey gave a shout, and forgetting his former loyalty to Ada, he pointed his finger at Mickser. 'So it was one of *your* family jilted her!' he cried. 'Oh, there's no doubt about it, you Dermodys are a dirty crowd!'

Mickser gave Molly a reproachful look. Betrayed by his own!

'Well, maybe he had good reasons,' he said darkly. 'After all, you couldn't blame him for not wanting to marry into a family that was cuckoo?'

This, Jamesey ignored. 'How do you know it wasn't *our* family that wouldn't let *her* marry *him*?' he demanded.

But Molly had stuck her fingers in her ears. 'Stop it. Both of you!' she cried. 'It doesn't matter what happened – it's so sad. To think of them living in the one town, seeing each other every day! And yet – Oh, it's *too* sad.'

'They didn't marry anyone else, either,' Annie said, looking at Molly.

'And they gave each other those lockets,' said Molly.

'And kept them till they died!' Annie put her arm around Molly's neck again.

'Still, I wonder why didn't they get married, Annie?' Molly said looking earnestly at Annie. The two girls seemed to be searching desperately for some explanation that would not rob the lovers of their lustre. 'Maybe they died young.'

But Annie had remembered something.

'I remember,' Annie cried suddenly. '*She* died young, I don't know anything about him, but Ada did. I know because my mother told me something that happened the summer before she died. Her sisters used to carry her out into the garden on sunny days, sofa and all, and bring out her meals on a tray, and one day when her sister was coming out with the tray, who did she see but *him*, Vinny! He was sitting on the end of the sofa talking to her. He'd climbed over the garden wall, and her sister knew he must often have done it. The sister was going to steal away and not let on she'd seen him, but she couldn't help hearing something he said. *You'll be better by the end of the summer, Ada,* he said. But do you know what *she* said. *Before the summer is gone, Vinny, I'll be gone.* Her sister wanted to rush over and tell Ada she mustn't *say* such things, but I suppose she knew it was true. And Vinny knew it too. Do you know what he said? *Ah Ada, if so, it'll be well for you!* Then he kissed her forehead and ran down the garden. I suppose he didn't want to go on living without her.'

Molly nodded. 'I know.' Her eyes were shining. 'How long did he live after her, I wonder. Oh, we must find out. I know. The dates will be on their tombstones. Let's go and find their graves!'

It was a great idea. It appealed to all of them.

'Come on,' they cried. 'Let's go.'

But Annie shook her head. 'They would have been buried in the old friary,' she said. 'We'd never find the graves. The headstones in there are all broken or buried in weeds.'

The children turned and looked at the friary wall. It was from there that weird cry came. At the mere thought of going in there their flesh crept.

'I bet we'd find them if we looked hard enough,' Molly insisted. 'It's so awful to think of them being forgotten. If we found their graves we could weed them – '

'We could get a scissors and cut the grass.'

'And put flowers over them.'

There was widespread enthusiasm as into their

minds came intoxicating visions of graves they'd seen in the New Cemetery, piled high with lilies and carnations that were marked out flower from flower by fronds of delicate maidenhair fern. Then their spirits sank again. Where would *they* get flowers? A few geraniums bloomed in a window box outside Morrisroes, and in every one of their back gardens a few nasturtiums and marigolds were to be found: but would they be let pick them?

'We could use leaves?' Molly cried. 'And ivy? And stuff like that!'

It was Mickser who settled the matter. 'We could make wreaths,' he shouted excitedly, 'and what do you call those things with glass domes over them you see on the graves in the New Cemetery – china flowers and china doves and silver rings, and crosses? We could make them.'

Immortelles? They didn't know what they were called, but many a time they'd put a foot through one and skinned their shins. Apart from the plaster doves and flowers they were only twisted wire. They weren't much different from rat-traps; just rusty cages of wire.

'They'd be easy to make,' Tim said jauntily.

They couldn't wait to get to work. Their fingers itched to twist wire and bend branches. There were no bounds now to their excitement. The Morrisroes were hopping like hailstones. But where would they get the doves, the crosses, and the entwined hearts?

'We might find something in our dung-hill, Mickser,' Molly said. Their dung-hill had often before provided untold treasure. 'Oh, come on. Let's hurry.'

They had wasted enough time already. The adults would soon be stirring into life. Already Duffy's old

collie dog had woken up and was ambling up the street
to them.

'Where are we going to work?' the Morrisroes
asked.

Mickser stared at them. He had assumed it would be
in his own yard.

'We have an old wheelbarrow in *our* yard,' Jamesey
said. 'It got caked with cement so it's not used any
more. We could have it to carry the wreaths.'

It seemed a deciding factor. 'All right so,' Mickser
agreed reluctantly. But when Molly and Annie started
off down the street, arm in arm, he suddenly called
Molly back. 'Wait a minute, Molly. Why should we
decorate the Duffy grave? Let us do our own.'

What had they been thinking about!

Molly and Annie unlocked their hands. And Ned
Conroy gave Duffy's collie a push with his boot.

In an instant, without picking sides at all, the two
sides were lined up, although, unnoticed, the Morrisroes had stuck together on Mickser's side. Next minute, wasting no further time on words, in tight formation and on opposite sides of the street, the children
set off to their respective encampments.

In the Dermody camp, which was quickly estab-
lished, there was an air of optimism and good cheer.
Mickser had called to mind an old wicker pram in the
loft over the grain store.

'It will be a lot easier to push than Duffy's wheelbarrow,' he said knowingly, 'and easier to hoist over
the wall. But we'd better divide up. Somebody will
have to get string – and wire. And somebody – you
two –' he nodded at the twins, 'you two – get the

leaves and the ivy.' He himself dashed up the loft ladder, but on the top step he stopped. Sounds of hammering were coming across the rooftops from the other yard. Optimism was not enough. 'Get a move on,' he yelled.

Immediately in Dermodys yard too there was the din of industry. And soon in the middle of the cobble-stones there was a mountain of leafy boughs and branches.

It was surprising, though, how long it took to make even one wreath – and a lopsided one at that. Ah well, it could go on the bottom. They set to work again. But the second wreath was not much better than the first. The third and fourth, however, weren't too bad. If only the wire wasn't so rusty. The girl's fingers were bruised and cut. Then Tim had a stroke of genius.

'If we had an old bike we could take off the wheels and tie the leaves and stuff on to it with string.'

But where would they get a bicycle wheel?

'We could take the wheels off the old pram!' Mickser cried, and he was just about to up-end it, when a new sound reached them across the roofs: the sound of an iron-shod wheel travelling over cobbles.

The Duffys were on the march.

The Dermody morale almost tottered, but with a deafening yell Mickser restored optimism.

'Quick! Throw all the stuff into the pram,' he commanded.

'But we're not finished, Mickser,' Molly wailed.

'We can finish them in the friary. We've got to find the grave yet!' Mickser glanced regretfully at the Morrisroes. 'I ought to have sent you two down ahead to start looking.'

To that wild and lonely place? The Morrisroes went white with fright. Molly patted them kindly on the back.

'Don't worry. It's too late now,' she said. She turned back to her cousin to reassure him also. 'The Duffys have to find their plot too, Mickser.'

Mickser's sharp ear however had caught a variation in the sound of the iron wheel. 'They've gone past the gap,' he said in astonishment. 'They've gone up the street. I knew they wouldn't be able to get that old barrow over the wall,' he gloated. Then his face fell. The Duffys did not employ a steady yard-man, like the Dermodys, but an old man came in occasionally to sweep the yard and tidy up their dung-hill in exchange for a hot meal. And this old man had a key to the friary where he sometimes set rabbit-traps. The Duffys must have got the key from him! 'They're going in by the gate! The easy way!' he said bitterly, but, next minute, grabbing the handle of the pram and pushing it ahead of him, he raced it out of the yard. 'Come on. We'll get our old pram over easily. Hurry. Hurry!' he yelled, as he raced the pram into the street, with the others after him, tossing in bits and pieces of greenery as they ran.

'I'll get up first,' Mickser said, when, a few seconds later they reached the gap in the wall. 'The rest of you stay below and hoist up the pram. Now!' he cried, when with the help of the ivy, which proved to be more of a help than a hindrance, giving him foothold and something to grip, he was safely on top. Sturdily then those below lent their weight, and like pall bearers, shouldered the old pram into the air. Once it was aloft, like sappers they all swarmed up.

Below them the old burial place was revealed to be a forest of dark nettles, with stalks of iron, and spikes for leaves. Undaunted Mickser had dropped down, and the weeds that looked so fearful were, after all, soft and sappy and they squelched under his feet.

'Now the pram!' he commanded, and when they'd sent it plunging downward, Tim and Ned and Molly jumped down themselves. The Morrisroes too got down without great difficulty.

The Dermodys were in possession of the field.

'The first thing we've got to do is find the grave,' Mickser said, as the others began to gather up some of the wreaths that had spilled out. 'Start searching. Spread out!'

His own heart sank though as he ploughed through the high weeds and the wild rank grass. Only a few tombstones showed above the nettles and they were splattered with white lichen that hid their lettering. Grabbing a fistful of grass Molly was frantically rubbing at an inscription on a stone near her. It was no use. Its message could not be read.

'Try another one, Molly,' Mickser cried, as he himself stumbled over the humpy ground. But Molly called him back in despair.

'It could be one of those humps,' she groaned, and Mickser saw that what he was stumbling over were graves too with the stones broken or sunk into the clay. He considered them for a minute.

'Ah, they'd only belong to the poor!' he said, and dismissed them.

At that moment, anyway, the Duffy wheelbarrow came rattling in through the gate at the other end of the graveyard, and the Duffys could be seen spreading out, scrambling around, like themselves, looking for their grave.

But soon the Dermodys heard frustrated shouts that seemed echoes of their own. Mickser gathered his forces around him.

'We're only wasting our time here,' he said. 'Our plot would have been a great big one with a great big tombstone.' Balancing himself on the broken stump of a small nameless stone, he surveyed the wilderness once more. 'Look! there's a big one over there.'

The tomb to which Mickser pointed was so magnificent it was hard to see how they hadn't spotted it at first, but, being close under the friary, a loop of ivy from the ruin had twined around it, almost obliterating it from view. That it was the biggest and best tomb in the place was however beyond dispute. To begin with it was marble. And to either side of it, through the drapery of ivy, there could be seen kneeling angels with bowed head and hands folded in marble prayer. Most important of all, however, on the top was a marble urn across which was laid a discreet fold of marble drapery.

'That's ours for certain,' Mickser declared.

In a mob the Dermodys ran through the weeds, the Morrisroes falling at every step, and Molly having each time to stop and pick them up. But when they got nearer to the tomb they saw with alarm that it was surrounded on all sides by spikey high black railings.

'That's because our family was so important,' Mickser explained. Being the first to reach it, he had clambered up on the coping stone. 'It's ours all right. I can read some of the names. Look! Malachi! James!' He turned to Molly. 'We had a grand-uncle Malachi, hadn't we? And a grand-uncle James?'

C

Ned and Tim and Molly were all up on the coping now too, and the Morrisroes stuck their heads between the bars. As a light breeze fluttered the young leaves near the top of the tomb, Molly made out another name.

'A-l-ph – ' she spelled. 'That must be our grand-uncle Fonsy. Fonsy is short for Alphonsus. And look. Cecelia. That's our great-aunt Celia; Celia for short.' But suddenly, with a thrill of absolute delight, through the trembling leaves she made out the name nearest to the top. 'Oh – oh – oh,' she breathed. 'Vincent! It's *him*. It's Vinny. See? His name is at the top, because he was the first to die.' Putting the inscription together letter by letter, she read it out ecstatically to Mickser – ' – and his beloved son, Vincent, died aged 26.'

There was general jubilation.

'But where is our grandfather's name? I don't see it,' Mickser whispered apprehensively to Molly.

'Oh, he wouldn't be buried here,' Molly explained. 'It's only the unmarried sons and daughters that go into the family plot.'

Satisfied, Mickser stepped down.

'Get the wreaths,' he ordered. In their anxiety to comply, the Morrisroes almost wrenched their heads off as they withdrew them from between the bars, and ran back to get the pram.

But at that moment a shout went up at the other end of the cemetery. Had the Duffys found their tomb? Not at all. The Duffys had only cheered because their old collie dog had started up a rat. And forgetting their quest, the Duffys, to a man, had joined in the rat-hunt.

Mickser heaved a sigh of relief. 'Now we'll have time to arrange the wreaths properly. Here, give me a leg up one of you and I'll get over the railing and fix them nice,' he said to the others.

But the Morrisroes who had arrived back with the pram, were nudging each other. One of them pulled at Molly's sleeve.

'The Duffys won't believe it's our tomb if they don't see the family name at the top.'

'Did you hear that, Mickser?' Molly said anxiously, but Mickser himself had already become aware that although names of grand-uncles and grand-aunts were plainly discernible, the name on the top of the tomb was obscured by a tangle of ivy so old and tough it might have been the parent of all the ivy in the cemetery.

'Shut up and do as I say. Give me a leg-up,' he said. 'Do you want the Duffys to come over before we're ready?'

'There's no need to worry about the Duffys,' said Ned. 'They're not bothering about us.'

And indeed, the barking of the old collie dog was getting further away, and fainter.

'They've lost the scent of the rat as well,' Mickser said with some satisfaction as, pushed from behind, he got over the railings.

Then, without wasting a second, running hard at it, he reached for the matted rope of ivy and dragged at it with all his strength. To no avail. The great rope of ivy remained firmly in place across the top of the marble slab as if it too were marble. Taking a deep breath, Mickser ran at it again. And again he dragged at it. After several attempts, however, he fell back exhausted. All his exertions had only scattered a few dead leaves and disturbed an earwig.

'It's no use, Mickser,' said Molly. 'You'll only hurt yourself.'

'I'll have one last go at it,' Mickser said, and this time when he rushed at the tomb, he leapt up and managed to lodge the toe of his boot in the fold of an angel's robe. Swinging himself upward, he threw an arm around the angel's neck.

'Oh Mickser, be careful,' Molly moaned.

But Mickser had crooked his free arm around the stem of the urn, and planted his two feet on the wooden rope of ivy.

'Mind out!' he cried, and loosening his hold, he let his whole weight come down on the tough old fibres.

This time with a creak the dry old fibre gave way, and as Mickser, with outspread arms, flew down through the air, under him went the great swathe of ivy, releasing the dust of a century of summers.

'Hurrah!' cheered the Dermodys. 'Hurrah.' And picking himself up, Mickser too was about to cheer when he turned and saw the name he had revealed.

'It's not ours at all,' he gasped, his head reeling, as he stared up at the large carved capitals which, protected for decades by the wad of ivy, now stood out sharp and clear as the day they were chiselled:

DUFFY

'Oh Mickser. It's Duffy's!' Molly couldn't bear to look at it any longer, her heart ached so for him.

But Mickser put out a hand between the bars of the railing and grabbed her by the arm. 'Take care would the Duffys hear you,' he hissed.

Too late. The Duffys had already heard. Arrested in

the rat-hunt, they were staring across the graveyard. 'Quick!' said Mickser to his men. 'Start throwing in the wreaths to me. Can't you see the Duffys think it is ours. Well, let them think it! Do you want them to find out it's not? That it's *theirs*? And that it was *us* found it for them!'

The next minute wreaths, branches, boughs, and fists-full of leaves went flying through the air and showered down inside the railing. And as fast as he could snatch them up Mickser laid them on the grave, indiscriminately hanging them on every angelic protuberance he could reach.

'Let up a few cheers,' he ordered. He himself was too busy to cheer.

The Dermodys' cheers were not a moment too soon, Jamesey Duffy had started to wade towards them. But the cheer stopped him. And seeing another shower of greenery hurtle through the air, he turned on his heel in disgust. A second later, whistling up the old collie dog, the Duffy contingent headed out towards the gate and left the field to the victors.

For a few minutes after the Duffys had gone out the gate, their defeated voices could be heard in the street. Then they were heard no more.

The Dermodys looked at each other. Standing in an island of trampled grass, they realised that although the sad evening sun was now slanting through the trees in the street outside, the massive clouds of ivy on the friary wall had already cast a deep shade over the lonely and silent place. It seemed that suddenly the old burial ground would plunge downward – and they with it – into a bottomless ocean of darkness.

'What time is it?' one of them asked fearfully, and

from the world outside, as if in answer, far, far away, a woman's voice was heard, raised in a thin, querulous call.

'That's our mother calling us!' the Morrisroes cried, together. And seeing that the Duffys had forgotten to close the gate, they scampered towards it.

'I'd better be going too!' Tim said, and when he slid away, Ned slid after him.

Soon only Molly and Mickser remained.

'They might have stayed and helped me out of here!' Mickser said sourly, but with Molly's help he did get out, although when he was standing beside her at last he was shivering.

'What's the matter, Mickser? Are you cold?'

'No,' he said. 'But let's get out of here.'

'What about the pram? Will we leave it till to-morrow?' Molly asked.

'It can stay here forever for all I care,' Mickser said fiercely, and he started for the gate.

Obediently Molly followed him, but as she went her eyes strayed over the sea of weeds where, like rocks in a rising tide, the gravestones, half submerged already, were about to be washed over altogether and drowned in shade.

'I wonder where her grave is? – Ada's I mean,' she said softly. Then she gave a little cry and came to a stand. 'Mickser! If that was the Duffy's tomb, how is it that all their great-uncles had the same names as our's? Malachi, Fonsy – even *Vinny*!' To Mickser's astonishment she began to laugh. 'Oh, wouldn't it be funny, Mickser, if it *was* our tomb after all?'

'But what makes you think that?'

'I don't know! I just thought how funny if it were!

And it could, you know. Our great-grandmother could have been a Duffy!' She clapped her hands. 'She was! Your mother once said our great-grandmother married one of her own shop-boys. His name must have been Dermody! Oh, isn't it funny, Mickser?'

Mickser didn't find it funny at all. It took him a good minute to work things out to his satisfaction.

'It must have been that shop-boy who brought the brains into our family,' he said then. And immediately he began feeling better. 'I bet he wasn't a real shop-boy. I bet he was a sort of foreman. That's why they put *his* name over the shop – so nobody would mix him up with those Duffys. The Duffys must never have been any good at all. Look at the way *they* let *their* business go downhill!' The more he thought of it now the better Mickser felt. 'Wait till we tell Jamesey,' he cried. How far had he gone? Could they catch up on him before he reached home? 'Come on quick, Molly,' he said, but she caught him by the arm.

'Mickser! If the Duffys and us are cousins, then *they* were cousins too, Ada and Vinny. Oh Mickser, that's why they couldn't get married. It wasn't anybody's fault. Oh, it's so sad.'

But Mickser was staring blankly at her.

'If they were cousins why would they *want* to get married? Wasn't being cousins enough for them?'

Molly hadn't thought of that. Mickser was right. What could be better? Why hadn't it been enough for Ada and Vinny? As he strode towards the gate she looked admiringly at him before she followed him obediently.

At the gate though, he stopped.

'Do you know what I think?' he said meditatively.

'I think that Ada was cuckoo too, like all the Duffys.' But as he spoke he caught sight of the key still in the padlock. 'Oh look, Jamesey forgot to give this back. Let's call and give it to him or he'll get into trouble. And we can tell him about the tomb.'

But after they locked the gate and were out in the street, a troubled expression came on his face. 'Do you think Jamesey was right about them not letting you come to see me at the school?'

'Oh, what does Jamesey know about it!' Molly said scathingly.

Mickser was not so confident. 'It's a pity you're not a boy, Molly. They couldn't stop you then.'

'Oh but Mickser, I'd *hate* to be a boy.'

'What?' Mickser couldn't believe his ears. 'Do you know what, Molly?' he said at last. 'I think *you're* cuckoo too, like the rest.' But he laughed with delight and caught her by the hand. 'I'll race you home,' he said. But they couldn't race holding hands, so he let go her hand.

'You'll have to give me odds,' she said.

'There! You see!' said Mickser. He gave her a length and they started to run.

Another summer day had ended.

Trastevere

The lights were changing at the corner of Madison and Sixty-ninth. To get across in time, Mrs Traske walked fast. Then, just as she reached the other side, she heard her name called. How nice to be hailed in the street like that on her first day back in New York! She turned expectantly. But the young man who called out had missed the light, and a river of cars now flowed between them. From the far bank he was waving frantically, and although she could not quite place him, Mrs Traske stood and waited, smiling reassurance.

Who was he? His face was certainly familiar, so she kept smiling. He was pleasant, eager and intelligent-looking. When the lights changed again, he bounded across.

'Mrs Traske! You remember me? Paul Martin. We met in Rome.'

Given an instant more, she'd have placed him. He was one of the young poets she'd met this summer. Rome was full of them, but this one was much the nicest.

'Of course!' she said. 'You took me to Trastevere – myself and my daughter.'

She'd been particularly grateful that he'd included Gloria; pretty young daughters were sometimes harder to entertain than people were aware. On the other hand, it must have been easier for him to be nice to Gloria than to a middle-aged novelist! Most of the poets in Rome were a bit contemptuous of Mrs Traske, especially when they heard she was staying on the Via Veneto. Fortunately, she had reached an age at which she was able to absolve herself for putting comfort before atmosphere. Their stay in Rome had been nearing an end when they met Paul. Hearing that they had never been across the river to Trastevere, he promptly offered to escort them. He planned an interesting afternoon, and – what they appreciated most – suggested they end the day with a visit to friends of his who had an apartment in a magnificent old medieval palazzo in the quarter.

'I thought you were still in Rome, Mr Martin,' she said, and, assuming that they were both going the same way, she started to walk on. But he did not move and did not let go of her hand. In fact, he gripped it tighter, and she realized that he was upset. The odd thing was that he seemed to connect her in some way with his distress.

'Oh, Mrs Traske, you don't know how good it was to look up and see you. I was in a telephone booth across the street. You of all people, I thought. I didn't know you were in New York. I just *had* to call out to you. You remember those friends of mine in Trastevere, the ones we had dinner with that evening – Simon Carr and Della?'

He was really very disturbed. He kept wiping his forehead.

'To look up like that and see you!' he cried. 'Someone who knew them! I'd only just heard, you see – just a minute before. I don't know any details yet, but oh

God, Mrs Traske, she killed herself – Della did – last night!'

'Oh, no!' Now she gripped *his* hand. 'How terrible. I can't tell you how sorry I am.' Sorry for him, she meant; he was so upset – the young woman she'd only met on that one occasion. Naturally, she was sorry for her, too, and for her poor husband. Yet her immediate sympathy went out to the young man in front of her. He was so *very* young in his grief. 'What happened?' she asked. 'Was there another woman?'

Paul was shocked. He threw up his hands in protest. 'He was hers, body and soul!' he cried.

'What was it, then?'

'That's what's so awful!' the young man cried. 'I don't know. I only heard she was dead. I was just going to put in a call to Rome – over there,' he said, nodding back, 'when I saw you. Oh, God, isn't it hard to believe? They were insanely in love. You must have seen that for yourself the evening in Trastevere.' With both hands now, he held on to her. 'What frightens me is that Simon may kill himself. He won't be able to live without her.' A wild look came into his eyes. 'And Della won't rest in the grave without him. She'll – '

But at this point Mrs Traske disengaged her hands. 'Now, don't talk rubbish,' she said. She was suddenly impatient with him. 'Let's walk on,' she said. 'Better still, come along to my hotel and have some lunch. It's quite near. You'll feel different when you've eaten something. We can talk.'

But Paul sprang away. 'I can't,' he cried. 'I've got to put in that call to Rome. I may have to go back there at once.' For another instant, he stood in front of her.

'Thank you again just for being here!' he cried. Then he was gone.

Shaken, Mrs Traske walked on alone. The poor girl, she thought – young woman, rather, for surely Della was a little older than her husband. Or was she? It may only have been his dependence on her that gave that impression. No matter, it was all very sad. As to Mr Martin's fears of a double suicide, however, she would not, quite frankly, give a fig for them. Widowed young herself, and having enough good sense not to make public by marriage a second, late but deeply satisfying relationship, she had her own concept of love.

What *had* happened, though? All she could recall of Della was that she was beautiful, with fine eyes and shining black hair. The evening Gloria and she had spent with the three young people ought to have been entirely enjoyable, but somehow it was not. Once or twice, it had seemed that Della was too dominating, but since the young men didn't seem to mind – quite the contrary – Mrs Traske had seen no reason to let it worry *her*.

Walking along Madison Avenue, she began to wonder. No more than Paul did she feel like lunch. She had an impulse to ring Mack, but she resisted it. He'd barely be back in his office, having met her at the boat and stayed to settle her in at the hotel. Anyway, she'd be seeing him for dinner. She stopped. She must be near Central Park. Ah, yes, she could see the tops of the trees. Perhaps she'd walk for a while in the sun there. According to her New York friends, Central Park was dangerous, but surely not in broad daylight? If one was to believe Mr Martin, not as dangerous as love! For although she'd snubbed him, Paul had made her think, with his fanciful notions of love. Crossing the avenue, Mrs Traske went in the direction of the Park. She'd miss out lunch altogether. After forty, it did no harm to skip a meal. She'd never been able to do that in Rome. There, she was hungry all the time. It made her ravenous just to walk down some of those narrow streets dedicated entirely to food – whole shops given over to one commodity: cheese, pasta, salami; stalls of fruit and vegetables arranged with as much regard to colour, shape, and size as the mosaics in the Vatican workshop. Passing them, her fingers used to itch to press a fleshy fig or a fat peach to see if it was as prime as it looked. But she was scared she'd set off an avalanche that would bury her up to the neck in apples and pears, figs, tomatoes, pomegranates, melons, aubergines. . . .

The day in Trastevere, they had eaten an excellent luncheon at her hotel, and yet they had no sooner crossed the Ponte Palatino than she was famished again, tantalised by the smells that came streaming out of apartment windows – the smell of hot cooking oil, garlic, oregano. All the walking they did made her twice as hungry. Paul had shown them everything – basilicas, crypts, palaces, fountains, piazzas. He was tireless. What they loved best were the narrow streets, like the Via dell' Atleta, that plunged them into the atmosphere of Trastevere, with orange peel underfoot and gaily coloured washing strung across overhead like bunting.

Thinking of what happened to her in one of those little streets, Mrs Traske had to smile. It was intensely hot and they were all perspiring, and so, although she was wearing only a light silk dress, she was relieved, really, when out of the sky a few drops of rain fell on her bare arm. She turned her face upward to receive them, 'As if,' Gloria said afterwards, laughing, 'as if you were a flower, Mother!' Only it wasn't rain! Overhead, high above, when she looked up she saw the bare bottom of a man-child, held out by his mother in her strong brown arms.

How they laughed. Then Paul tactfully suggested that perhaps they ought to be getting on, as Della would be expecting them. She liked to eat early, because she had a job, he explained; she was always ready to eat the minute she got home from the office.

'Oh, we mustn't keep her waiting,' Mrs Traske said, for from the first she had assumed they were going to eat in the apartment. That seemed the whole point of the visit. They had seen the outside of enough old palazzos.

'Wait till you see their apartment!' Paul cried. 'I told you, didn't I, it's in one of the oldest palazzos in Rome, with balconied windows and studded doors – and they have a terrace garden on the roof. There it is!' he announced as they entered a *piazzale* off which ran a street as narrow as a gully.

Impressed, they stood and stared at the massive ornamented façade that projected over the thoroughfare.

'There are disadvantages, of course, as you can see,' Paul said when they got nearer and an acrid odour assailed them from the brimming garbage bins that had not yet been emptied. Like cornucopias, the bins spilled out a largesse of lobster claws, fish heads, egg-shells, decayed flowers, and the pulp of rotted fruit. And from the lavish heap, as they went past, a swarm of flies rose into the air with an iridescent glitter, hissing like geese.

'Sorry for that,' Paul said easily. 'It's the price for

living in the quarter. But look at that carving!' He pointed up at the magnificent portico.

They were having trouble, however, getting past the garbage bins, and in the hallway itself they had to push their way through a horde of small children playing on the marble floor and the lower steps of the great marble staircase. The hallway was infested with children. They were very sweet, very appealing, but she had to hold her skirts clear of their grubby little fingers. When they reached the stairs she had to laugh out loud at one small fat infant who was trying to get up the great marble step. His diaper, heavy with urine, hung down under him like an udder, and left a wet track after him wherever it touched the steps.

'Like a snail!' said Gloria, and she lifted him to one side so they could pass, although in fact the wide staircase was so broad they could easily have got past him. All three of them could have gone up it abreast. A magnificent staircase. And on the walls, set in plaster, there were wonderful ceramic medallions, although elsewhere on the plaster, up as high as they could reach, the children had been busy with chalk and crayon.

'I don't advise looking too closely,' Paul cautioned uneasily. And, indeed Mrs Traske had just seen a very crude drawing. It wasn't all the work of children, not by any means. Not wishing to embarrass the young man, she launched into a generality. 'Graffiti fascinate me,' she said. 'I read a most interesting article on the subject recently.'

The words were hardly out of her mouth when a door opened overhead and a voice called down. 'What kept you? We're starving.'

Such familiarity was warming, and the Traskes hurried up, but when Mrs Traske got to the landing she couldn't help stopping again and exclaiming at the rich Venetian red of the walls that was so well set off by the pure white of the door and the pedimented architrave. 'What glorious colour!' she cried to the young man standing on the landing – Simon?

He smiled. 'It was extravagant of us to decorate the landing, because it doesn't belong to us legally. It's supposed to be communal, but as we're at the top we took a chance and did the landing, too, when we were doing up the rest.'

Gloria and Paul had joined them.

'I always say,' said Paul, 'that this landing sounds a trumpet for what is to come!' Stepping past Simon, he threw the door of the apartment fully open.

At the sight of the room within, Mrs Traske gasped and gave another rapturous exclamation.

'You sound surprised, Mother,' Gloria said sharply. 'Mr Martin did try to prepare us.'

Mrs Traske smiled at her daughter, grateful to her for helping her transform her surprise into more tactful terms of appreciation.

'But how could anyone be prepared for such dramatic colours?' Mrs Traske said quickly. 'That glowing ruby, and now this green. It's as green as the campanile,' she added when, stepping into the room, she saw the dome of Santa Maria in Cappella through one of the great windows at the far end. She turned back to her host. 'Is your wife an artist?' she asked.

For no reason that she could see, Simon and Paul both laughed – quite loudly, too.

'Well, then, it is the room of a poet,' she murmured. The room demanded a fitting tribute.

At this point, the door of a kitchenette opened and a young woman came out. Della? Like her husband, she dispensed with greetings and joined at once in the conversation. Again, the familiarity had the effect of putting the Traskes at ease. 'The room of a poet?' the young woman repeated, questioningly, and she looked around it like a stranger. 'You should have seen the room where he lived before we were married,' she said, but she took her husband's arm and squeezed it affectionately. She nodded at the prints on the wall. 'The prints were Simon's, of course,' she said. 'I only reframed them. And the old desk was his – I just had it stripped and waxed. And the books are his.' But she frowned slightly, because some of the books looked a bit ragged. She hugged his arm tighter. 'I think the colour was your idea, too, wasn't it? Or was it Paul's?' She reached out and drew Paul to her. 'I only paid for things!' She turned to Mrs Traske. 'Perhaps you're right,' she said. 'Perhaps it is the room of a poet, but with the tone raised an octave or two – by money.'

The mention of money in this way would have made Mrs Traske uncomfortable if it were not that the young men – both of them – were so obviously delighted with Della.

'I must tell you,' Paul said. 'Della has one of the best jobs in Rome.' He laughed. 'That's why they came here – and me, too.'

Did he live with them? Mrs Traske wondered. This room was so spacious there could not be very much sleeping accommodation beyond it.

Paul seemed to read her mind. 'I don't live *with* them,' he said. 'I only live *off* them.'

At this, again all three laughed, and Mrs Traske

D

laughed with them. She could see, though, that Gloria found Della rather overpowering. What a strong personality. Standing there in the middle of her beautiful room, with the two young men linked to her, she suddenly presented an extravagant image to the mind of Mrs Traske – an image of a Maypole, festooned with ribbons, which, as they gyrated, bound the young men closer and closer to her.

'Simon, aren't you going to offer them a drink?' Unlinking herself, Della picked up an empty glass that had evidently been her own, then put it down again. 'I won't have any more,' she said, and it was hard not to feel this was a reprimand to them for being late. All the same, Mrs Traske and Gloria took the drinks that, without choice, were offered to them, and Mrs Traske began at once to sip hers as an example to Gloria, who loathed Campari and found it as hard to swallow as cough syrup.

'It was good of you to come,' Della said then, unexpectedly. 'We've heard a lot about you from Paul.'

Mrs Traske had started to give the self-deprecatory smile with which she usually acknowledged over-facile praise of her work when Della continued. 'About your generosity to young people, I mean,' she said.

How glad Mrs Traske was then for those frank admissions concerning Della's salary, because if money had been in short supply she would have thought the young woman was leading up to a request for a loan. As things were, it did cross her mind that they might be expecting something other than money from her. She turned to Simon. 'I regret to say I haven't read any of your poetry,' she murmured.

Della took her empty glass. 'How could you?' she

said. 'It's never been published,' and before Mrs Traske could say anything more she put up her hand as if in warning. 'Don't suggest reading it in manuscript,' she cried, 'unless you are an Egyptologist or a hierogly-phist,' and, reaching out, she joined the two young men to her again. 'They call themselves writers, and no one can read their writing.' She laughed. 'And they can't spell.' She laughed again. 'They don't even know the meaning of words. Do you know what this fellow here thought?' She hugged Paul tighter to her. 'He thought temerity meant timidity! And this fellow here' – she hugged her husband's arm – 'this fellow thought a hysterectomy was a lobotomy! Not that one can blame him too much for that; the medieval phil-osophers all thought the womb was the centre of the emotions.' She let them go. 'Oh, they are hopeless cases. I don't know what they'd do if they didn't have me to look after them.'

And, indeed, to Mrs Traske it was beginning to seem as if she did give them strength. In the large room where she and Gloria stood apart as separate people, the three young people seemed to stand as closely grouped together as when they were linked.

'Take the girl's glass,' Della said to Simon. 'And if we're ready, let's go and eat.'

But it was over to the door through which they had come in she walked, and, opening it, she led them out on to the landing.

'Are we not going to eat here?' said Mrs Traske. Too late she knew she'd let slip that she was dis-appointed. She hadn't seen the room properly, hadn't looked at the prints or the books, and, above all, she hadn't had time to look out of the window at the wonderful view of Trastevere. She glanced regretfully around.

'Do you mind?' Della said, almost offensively, and she held the door open. Mrs Traske couldn't help feeling she'd been put under a compliment.

'We'd be happy to take pot luck, you know,' she said nervously. 'Gloria wouldn't mind giving a hand. She's quite a good cook. She makes a delicious omelette.' The truth was that after months of living in hotels and eating out, she herself would have enjoyed helping with a meal. She thought again of the vegetable stalls, and she could almost feel the snap of young beans under her fingers, and the swish of spinach.

Della however had turned away. 'We never eat in the apartment,' she said. 'There's a trattoria in the cellar of the palazzo – you must have seen the sign in the hallway when you were coming up here. We eat there every night – in fact we only eat up here on very rare occasions.'

'Sad occasions, not joyful,' Paul explained quickly. 'If one of them is sick, or something like that.'

'The smell of cooking hanging around the apartment all evening would disgust me,' Della said.

Still Mrs Traske was not happy. 'We shouldn't have come for a meal at all,' she murmured.

'But why should you think that?' Simon said. 'It's not that Della is tired or anything; it's just that we can afford to eat out – because of her job.'

'That's right,' Della said more graciously. 'If it weren't for my job, we probably wouldn't be able to eat at all!' She saw Gloria look surprised, and she gave a little laugh. 'Don't worry,' she said, and she nodded at her husband. 'He pays in other ways.' She paused. 'He washes the nappies.' When both Mrs Traske and Gloria failed to conceal their surprise at this, she shrieked with laughter. 'Figuratively speaking!' she cried. 'We haven't any little nappies.'

Mrs Traske looked nervously at Simon. As both he and Paul laughed, however, she tried to laugh, too. Gloria only stared.

'Don't worry,' Paul whispered reassuringly as they went down the stairs. 'Della knows what she's doing. Other people's extravagances are her economies.'

But it was no longer her social obligations that concerned Mrs Traske. 'Are they long married?' she asked.

'About three months,' Paul said. He leaned closer. 'They were living together for some time in London, but when Della got this great job in Rome they decided to get married.' He lowered his voice still more. 'I don't think Simon liked the idea of marriage at first – that's what Della meant about the little nappies – but he knew he couldn't live without her.' He grinned. 'I can hardly live without her myself. I'm over here on a grant, and I'm staying in a good enough pensione, but – well, I spend all my time here in their apartment. I'm afraid I lean on her, too. She's that kind of person. I'd heard of people like her before, but I never met one – people whose strength is a kind of magnet for people like Simon and me, who are pretty helpless when it comes to living. It's true!' he said when Mrs Traske looked quizzically at him.

They were at the bottom of the great stairs, and now she could see that there was a greasy sign on the wall and a steeper, darker stair leading down to the trattoria in the cellar.

The trattoria was small but packed with people. When Della appeared, however, the little fat patron, his face glistening with sweat, ran forward at once to meet them, as if he'd been rolled at them like a ball, and began to bow them toward the only empty table in the room, way at the back near the service doors.

'*Signore! Signora!*' He beamed until suddenly he saw Mrs Traske and Gloria. Thinking them a separate party, he was thrown into confusion, and more sweat broke from his face – it might have been rubbed all over with oil. For a moment, it was as if he were some lower form of life that would divide in two, both halves able to go forward and bestow welcomes alike on the two parties at the same time. But this being impossible, he clapped his hands and, summoning a waiter in a long lank apron down to his boots, ordered him to attend on the strangers. '*La carta per gli Inglesi!*' he cried. Then, as he realised that they were together, one single party, a beatific smile of relief broke over his face. '*Momento!*' he cried to the waiter. '*Carta per tutti.*' Without waiting to be obeyed, he dashed over to a service table and rushed back with a fistful of menus so greasy and wine-stained they were positively succulent, and dealt them out.

'*Prego.*' He gave one to Della. '*Prego.*' One to Mrs Traske. '*Prego, prego, prego,*' he cried, dealing one to each person. But the next instant he gathered them up again and discarded them. Like a conductor disdaining the score, he began to extol from memory the delights of his kitchen. '*Pollo al diavolo? Saltimbocca? Abbacchio*

alla cacciatora? 'Tonight it is tender' – he bowed to
Gloria – 'like the eyes of the *Signorina*.' Then, con-
spiratorially, he lowered his voice. '*Osso buco*,' he whispered. 'Tonight it is – ' He stopped, and, placing a kiss
on his fat fingers, he blew it heaven-ward. As there was
still no response, he was silent for a moment. Then he
raised his voice again. 'Steak!' he cried. Just the one
word. But now he was no longer a restaurateur; he was
a generalissimo. He held up his hand for their attention. '*Momento!*' he cried, and he stumped off through
the service doors. When he emerged again, it was tri-
umphantly, with a piece of raw steak on the palm of his
hand; blood from it oozed through his fingers. 'Never
a steak like this,' he said solemnly. 'Never!'

All except Mrs Traske and Gloria gave the steak a
close scrutiny, Della even lifting it up and turning it
over. But Simon winked at Gloria, and put on a face of
mock dismay. 'What good is that when there are five
of us,' he said.

'*Scusi?*' Angelo did not immediately catch that a joke
was meant. Then, offended, he frowned. 'I speak of the
little Florentine heifer from which we take the steak!'
he said with dignity. '*Molto* steak, *molto!*' he corrected.
And, assuming that an order had been given, he handed
the meat to the waiter. His hands free, he clapped them
commandingly. 'Steak *per tutti!*' he cried.

Mrs Traske would have preferred an omelette, and
Gloria loathed steak. To make matters worse, Della
had called 'Underdone!' after the little patron.

'*Capisco!*' Angelo cried, and was about to scuttle off.
'But I – ' said Gloria.

Angelo stopped.

It was Simon, though, who had arrested him. 'Wait

a minute, Angelo,' Simon said. 'Tonight I think I'll try the *osso buco*.'

'Simon!' Della was astonished. 'You know you hate sloppy dishes.'

'*Osso buco*,' Simon repeated.

'Simon!' Della caught him by the arm. 'It will take ages – twenty minutes, at least – you know that? You don't want to wait that long.'

But Angelo was all eagerness to comply. 'For the *Signore* – no!' he cried. Prudently measuring the distance between him and the other tables, he lowered his voice. 'For the one who comes in off the street, yes, maybe, but *per il cliente – il Signore* – no, no. I fix it myself, at once.' He held up five fat fingers. '*Cinque minuti.*'

Della sat back. 'Well, bring ours when it's ready, Angelo – without waiting,' she said. She still looked puzzled. She turned to Mrs Traske. 'I don't believe I've ever known him to eat *osso buco*,' she said. Then, as Angelo was hurrying away, she called again, 'Underdone!'

Mrs Traske looked at her. No matter what the two men said, it seemed to Mrs Traske that Della did look tired. It could, of course, have been that she was hungry, because she had picked up a roll and begun to pluck out the soft inner dough.

'It's all very well for Simon and Paul,' she said. 'They lunch here, too – that is to say, if they get up for lunch at all.' Suddenly she looked strangely at Mrs Traske. 'What time do you begin your day?'

Surprised, Mrs Traske hesitated. 'Do you mean when I'm at home, or do you mean here in Rome? This morning, we didn't get up very early, because Paul warned us that we'd have a tiring day trudging around and seeing the sights.'

As Paul nodded, Della gave him an affectionate smile. 'Did you really show them everything?' she asked him. 'For you the day must have been exceptionally exacting.'

Paul laughed. 'Della doesn't think writing poetry is work at all,' he said.

'But she married a poet!' Mrs Traske said, feeling she had to defend the young woman.

It was a shock to find that instead she had annoyed her. 'I married a man – a man like any other man, I hope,' Della said sharply. 'I don't see why allowances should be made for him on account of his work. I'd be insulted if anyone made allowances for *me* on account of *mine*.'

'Oh, but – ' Mrs Traske began, when Gloria spoke up.

'Mother never expects allowances to be made for her, either,' she said hotly. 'But it's not the same as if she was just a lawyer or a pediatrician! When she's working she can't sleep and she can't eat and she gets upset over nothing. Writers are sometimes working when we think they're only standing looking out of the window! Didn't you know that?' she demanded crossly, and so like a small child her mother had to smile.

Fortunately, Della was not offended. On the contrary, she was amused. 'Do you mean that Simon here may be working when he's fast asleep at three o'clock in the afternoon?'

Gloria was not to be put off so easily. 'That's not fair,' she said. 'It *is* true his mind could be working –

unconsciously – and that takes a lot out of a person. The artist has always been regarded as a sacrificial figure and – '

'Gloria!' Mrs Traske just couldn't let her go on. 'She has been reading *The Wound and the Bow*,' she said to Della by way of apology.

Della brushed the apology away, however, and actually encouraged the girl. 'Go on,' she said. 'I'm interested. I take it that you feel my husband here is some special kind of being.'

Uncertain suddenly, Gloria looked for help from her mother, but the ice was thin; it would never bear the weight of two.

'Well,' said Gloria slowly, to gain time as she searched around in her mind. 'Writers and artists, and people like that – they do have special insights, don't you think?'

Della looked at her with a grave expression. Then, equally gravely, she looked at Simon. 'You think' – she paused – 'you think he may be some kind of a nut?'

Here Paul exploded with laughter, and Mrs Traske would have laughed if she weren't a bit anxious about Gloria, who could easily have burst into tears.

The girl felt too strongly for that, though. 'Put it that way if you like!' she cried. 'I suppose some people *do* think poets are nuts. Just because they don't measure success by money!' Her cheeks were flaming.

And Della was apparently touched. She laid a hand on the girl's arm. 'How nice it must be to have you for a daughter,' she said with real sweetness, but then she turned sharply to Mrs Traske. 'Of course, it's true you writers *are* above money, isn't that so?' she said, and to Mrs Traske's amazement her eyes travelled – really quite insolently – over her dress, and came to rest on her opal-and-diamond brooch.

Compelled now to speak up herself, Mrs Traske looked Della in the eye. 'My husband was a stock-broker,' she said.

At that moment, luckily, the steaks arrived.

'Let's begin, shall we?' Della said when, except for Simon, they were all served. 'Poor Simon,' she said. 'I told you it would take twenty minutes. Now aren't you sorry you're not one of the common herd?'

'*Momento. Momento,*' Angelo clucked.

'Go easy, Gloria. You'll get indigestion,' Mrs Traske said trying to slow her down, although she sympathised with her motives for gulping it off – the steaks were positively blue.

Slow as they all went – and even Della ate slowly – they were finished before Angelo came back proudly bearing, breast-high, the platter of *osso buco*.

'It looks good,' Gloria said as she handed her empty plate to a waiter.

'It smells delicious, Simon,' Della said, and as Angelo took her plate she reached out and snatched her fork. Leaning across the table, she stuck the fork into the *osso buco*. To the astonishment of all of them, Simon, who had just picked up his own fork, threw it down on the plate with a clatter.

'Why, Simon, what's the matter?' Della cried. 'I only wanted . . .'

Simon didn't look at her. He pushed his plate across the table. 'If you wanted it, why didn't you order it? There. You can have it.'

'But Simon!' Della was so taken aback she held her

fork in the air, half-way to her mouth. Unnoticed, the meat fell from the prongs. Then, quietly and carefully, she picked it up and put it on her side plate and laid the fork back on the table, straightening it as if she were laying a place setting. 'I only wanted to see if it tasted good,' she said, in a voice that for her was low and indistinct.

'I don't want it,' Simon said.

Stupefied, they all stared.

'Will you have a steak, then?' Della asked.

'No. I'm not hungry,' Simon said. 'You eat it if you want it.'

Della looked down at the full plate in front of her. 'But I don't want it,' she said. 'I had what I ordered – I only . . .' Then she didn't attempt any more apology. 'Don't be absurd, Simon. We'll wait for our dessert until you've eaten. Eat it up,' she said, pushing back the plate. She turned in exasperation to Paul. 'What's the matter with him?' she cried. 'Tell him not to be childish.' She turned to her husband. 'Eat it up, Simon.'

Simon, however, had leaned back and was calling Angelo. 'Take this away,' he said, pointing to the plate.

Angelo stared at him.

'Don't worry, Angelo,' Della said quickly. 'It's just that he's not hungry.' As the patron took up the plate but stood uncertainly with it held low, like a collection plate, she jumped up from her chair and whispered something into his ear. 'Go along, Angelo,' she said then, out loud, 'and bring our dessert.' She turned back to those at the table. 'What will you have? Fruit? Cheese?' To Gloria she spoke kindly, as if she were a child. 'How about a *cassata* for you?'

Embarrassed, they all nodded acceptance of what apparently was decreed for them.

It hardly seemed possible that the awkwardness would pass. Thinking of it now, Mrs Traske, walking in the sunlight, felt that there, in that incident – if anywhere – was a hint of why the young woman had killed herself. But no. As she recalled it, after that things had gone well. Nothing more was said about the *osso buco*. Simon was suddenly in better form. Indeed, the next quarter of an hour was the most pleasant of the whole evening. They were all soon at ease, and for the first time Simon showed a real interest in the Traskes and their travels. 'How long are you going to be in Rome?' he'd asked.

'I'm not sure yet,' she'd replied without much thought, eager only to keep the conversation on a safe topic. 'We intended going to Milan the day after tomorrow, but somehow or other, on the way here from Florence, we missed out on Viterbo, and I'm told – '

'Oh yes, yes. You can't leave without seeing Viterbo.' He laughed. 'Though, mind you, I was only there once, years ago, and I didn't see much of it. I was drunk. Very drunk.' He turned to Paul. 'You remember that day?' He turned back to Mrs Traske. 'We'd hired an old car and we were supposed to turn it in in Rome, but we didn't really expect it would last out the trip. We were driving along when we saw the sign for Viterbo, and felt we ought to see it, so we turned off the main road. We thought we might eat there. But after we'd driven down some of the old streets – Viterbo is *all* old streets, and they're *all* crooked, *all* dark, *all* damp, even on the hottest day – well, we didn't think much of it, and we certainly didn't feel like eating there, and so we were trying to find the way out again when the old car gave a jolt. Blump it went. And then blump again. Blump, blump, blump. Paul, you remember?'

Paul was convulsed with laughter. 'Go on!' he cried.

Simon went on. 'Can you imagine a flat tyre in a place like that? We looked at each other in despair, threw up our hands, and decided to drive on. Blump we went, blump, blump, blump, blump, blump. We began to think we'd punctured all four tyres. And then to make things more hectic, although when we first drove into the place it was like a city of the dead, not a living soul in sight, *now* from all sides people appeared. Men, women, children – especially children. The children started running after us, shouting and yelling. I stepped on the gas. In a backward place like that, a pack of children is as bad as a pack of wolves. We tried to put a bit of distance between us and them, and I thought we were getting up speed when all of a sudden the kids dropped back. They stopped dead, in fact, and huddled together. The last I saw of them they were staring with their mouths wide open. Then I was jerked back as all of a sudden the ground went from under the car. Next thing there was a loud smack and a great almighty splash. We hadn't a puncture at all. We'd driven down a flight of steps into the river. That was all!'

'Oh, Simon, you never told me that story,' Della said. 'I want to go there. I want to see those steps.'

She was laughing so happily Mrs Traske thought that perhaps after all no harm had been done by the incident of the *ossobuco*.

'How did you get the car out of the river, Mr Carr?' Gloria asked.

Dear girl. How they laughed at her.

'You must never look beyond the end of a good story, Gloria,' Paul said. 'Your mother could have told you that.'

They were all happy again.

'We certainly won't miss Viterbo after this,' Mrs Traske said, and she began to draw on her gloves. 'Which means we will be staying another day in Rome, so why don't you all have lunch with me tomorrow at my hotel?'

'But Della doesn't eat lunch,' Simon said in dismay.

'I have a snack at the canteen,' Della explained.

'Oh, what a pity,' Gloria said, and Mrs Traske turned to Paul, whom Angelo had released from his chair by pulling the table out from the wall. 'Perhaps you and Simon . . .' she began.

Uncertainly, both men looked at Della.

'Why not?' Della said. 'It would be a change for Simon.' She paused. 'A change from lying in bed, I mean.'

Once again for a moment, Mrs Traske's heart sank at what sounded to her like an unnecessary gibe, but again the young men seemed to see it in some other light, because they both laughed. It seemed settled that the young men would come to lunch.

Meanwhile, they were moving towards the stairs, and Paul had run up the steps to call a taxi.

'What time?' Simon said.

'How about noon?' she said, and she was just about to compliment Angelo on the meal as he bowed them out, his face now in the heated room glistening as if he was sweating glycerin.

Della, who had been looking at the little patron, suddenly turned to her husband. 'Simon! I forgot. You can't go. You've got to lunch *here* tomorrow. Isn't that right, Angelo?' she asked, smiling at him.

'*Si, si, Signora.*' Angelo bobbed his head up and down.

Della reached out and patted him. 'You are a dear, Angelo,' she said, before she took Simon's arm and began to move towards the door. 'Angelo is keeping your *osso buco* for your lunch tomorrow,' she said. 'Those sloppy dishes improve by keeping – the flavour comes out with standing overnight.' Then she turned to Mrs Traske and put out her hand. 'You'll be in Rome again,' she said indifferently.

Simon said nothing, and somehow Mrs Traske didn't look at him as she shook hands. He had pulled away from Della, Mrs Traske saw out of the corner of her eye. She started to go up the dark stairs, and when she reached the street Paul was there with the taxi. She thought it best to let the others explain about the lunch to him. She and Gloria got into the car.

As it drove away, she looked back at the three of them standing on the kerb. Simon seemed taller than she'd realised, and Della was really quite small. That Maypole image had been absurd, she thought, and even Paul's description of her as a tower of strength didn't seem right any more. Mrs Traske stopped. Was it possible that Della wasn't strong at all – that she had all the time been taking strength, not giving it as the young men thought?

Mrs Traske was surprised to find that her eyes had filled with tears. She wiped them away and looked around for a seat. She'd exhausted herself with her efforts to probe human motive, and now she felt curiously lonely. She sighed, and looked at her watch. She never liked to ring Mack during office hours, but perhaps just this once she might do so. He might slip out for a cup of coffee with her. It would be nice to meet him at this banal time of day and not wait for the more circumspect hours of evening.

She sighed again. Life was so short. And she remembered something Mack had once said, to which she had not attached importance at the time. She had said that she did not see much point in getting married at their age, when they had not much left to give each other, and he had shaken his head in disagreement.

'At least we do not diminish each other,' he said.

Were they making a mistake, she wondered, she and Mack? In spite of how often they thrashed things out and discarded the idea of marrying – laughed at the mere notion – perhaps after all . . .

She had come to a gate leading back into the street, and there would be a phone booth close by. She'd call Mack anyway. Even on the phone he was able to cheer her up – make her happy, make her laugh. She walked faster. For a woman of her years, her step at that moment was light.

E

Asigh

Only once in all the years did he say anything about it, and that was a few days before he died. He was lying so still she thought he was asleep, but his eyes were open and staring at the rags on her leg.

'Does it trouble you much?' he asked. That was all, but her fear of him flared up as fierce as the day he struck her. And ill though he was, helpless – dying – she wanted to tell a lie and say it didn't trouble her at all. Perhaps she felt that to exonerate him might have freed him from the guilt that smouldered behind his terrible eyes. But the saturated rags wrapped round her leg would show up the lie.

'Only a bit, Father,' she said. 'Not much.'

'It was the brass buckle did it,' he said, speaking as if it were only yesterday. It was sort of an apology. She knew that. But not for his action! No! Never for that! Only for its unfortunate outcome. 'There must have been verdigris on that buckle,' he said. 'And verdigris is poison. If your mother was alive she'd have put something on the cut to take the poison out of it.' He kept looking at her leg and feeling awkward she moved away. She was going out of the room, when he rapped on the table by his bed. 'Why didn't you know it was poison?' he said. 'Well, you know it now!'

Then, as unexpectedly as he had opened them, he

66

closed his eyes again, and whatever need had made him break the silence of a lifetime must at last have been satisfied because he was asleep almost at once. She went back and stood looking down at him. He was in one of the heavy, unnatural sleeps that of late came down so often upon him. Soon sleep would close in upon his consciousness altogether. He couldn't last much longer. It would be all over then, the long imprisonment of her life with him. But she took no pleasure in the thought. Her brother Tom was as much to be pitied, or more, and he never complained. Lately the thought of her father's death passed through her mind with greater and greater frequency. Now, to banish it, she looked out at the fields that washed up almost to the hall door.

Closed in by summer, the fields were deeper and lonelier than ever, and the laneway that led out to the road was narrowed by overhanging briars and the wild summer growth of bank and ditch. Away in a far field down by the river her brother Tom was scything weeds. He was cutting away with an easy rhythmical movement. As she watched he stopped to put a new edge on the blade, and when he reached down for the whetstone she was startled to see how stiff and awkward he was. The man on the bed was suppler than him! A feeling of pity for Tom's dried and wasted years assailed her, but her leg had begun to throb again. It may have been that her father's words had wakened the pain. She put her hand to it. The pain was so bad it might have been the moment it happened, when he'd come upon her suddenly in the churchyard, talking with one of his own workmen, and in the sight of all the other stragglers, raised the head-collar in the air and swung it over her. Sparkling like a star in the day-sky the buckle had held her eyes for an instant before it darkened down upon her.

She'd fallen with the pain. And as she fell, she saw Jake take to his heels across the slabstones. But her father didn't give him a glance.

'Get up!' he'd said to her. 'Get up!' And as if she was a beast that had fallen, he struck her again to rise her. Not that he was a man who ever ill-treated a beast. Nor for that matter had he ever before objected to her having a word with a man. Indeed, he used to give her a coarse encouragement.

'You'd better watch your step in that jacket, girl,' he'd say of an evening when she was going out for a walk, even when she was too young to know what he meant. She often thought there might have been a queer meaning in his words, but if so she didn't want to uncover it. Indeed she used to laugh and run out-doors. And as for some of the dresses he bought her in the town when he'd go to the Fair, the neighbours' tongues used to clack at them.

'It's easily seen you have no mother, you poor child.' That was said to her more than once when her father had decked her out as fancily on plain ordinary days of the week as if it was a Sunday or a holy day. She couldn't play in the kind of dresses he bought her. Maybe that was how she got into the habit of standing about drawing looks from the boys in the schoolyard, and later, bolder looks from their own workmen, particularly Jake. It was behind her father's back for most part that she got those looks – specially from Jake, but her father knew about them and he never seemed to mind. She used to think he put some construction of his own on them, that they were a measure of something in his mind.

In her own mind that was all they were too, a measure of her attraction. Obscurely she knew, even then, that nature made use of small affinities to prepare the heart for the final, the fatal, the immortal affinity of love.

One day, a week before she was seventeen, when a spanking back-to-back trap drove into the yard, she was drawn to the doorway by something more compelling than curiosity.

'The name is Mallon – Tod Mallon,' the owner of the trap said, jumping down and going to meet her father who'd come out of the cowshed at the sound of the wheels rattling over the cobbles. She stayed where she was, standing at the yard-door. But Mallon had seen her. And if she knew in that instant what she had been waiting for, there was a look in his eyes that made her feel that he, too, had come to the end of some kind of waiting. In his case, though, it had been a longer wait than hers, he being a mature man. She heard him announce to her father that he had just bought the farm next to them. It was as big a farm as their own.

'Both divisions,' he said proudly, 'and it's the best of land. But it was over-stocked at the back-end of the year, and I'll be short of hay. I'm told you have a field of second-crop meadow for sale on foot?'

'The hay will be for sale all right,' her father said slowly, 'but I was thinking of making it up myself.' His shrewd eyes were trying to sum up the stranger, but afterwards she knew it was for other reasons than she'd thought at the time. In his mind her father had paired them up, herself and Mallon in that first

moment. Because her father too had been waiting –
waiting, for someone like Tod to come along as a
husband for her.

Of course at that time all was looks. In the silent
fields living close to the mute beasts, there was more
meaning to be got out of looks and glances than there
was for people in the towns. She used to think sometimes that for people like them – her, and her father
and Tod – words only ran alongside looks like the
song of the stream runs alongside the meaningful
ripples. All the same there were times when words had
their full potency, and never more than when men
were making a deal.

'Will you give me the first refusal one way or another?' Mallon asked.

'Would you like to have a deal here and now?'

'That depends on what you're asking?' Mallon said.

'How much is the worth of it?' her father asked.

The two men had moved across the yard towards
where a gate led into the meadow. Her father leant back
against the gate, facing away from it, for he knew every
blade of grass that was in it; but Tod Mallon leant forward and looked deep into the grass that swelled like a
sea, and was as green as the sea, with not a blotch of
blossom marring it, from mearing to mearing, but only
darker clots of green where cow pads had coarsened
the growth. And she, standing to one side of the men,
could see how Mallon coveted the rich grass, and how
he coveted the skill that had brought a crop like it out
of their light gravelly land. But above all, she saw how
his eyes took pleasure in its rippling waves.

Then the bargaining broke out again involuntarily.

'Well, what is it worth?' her father asked.

'To me? Or to you?'

'What's the differ?' Her father seemed surprised.

'Oh, there's a big difference,' said Mr Mallon. 'And what's more, I'd say you're a man that sets a steep value on anything you have to offer.'

Her father laughed. And seeing she had come up to them, he flung his arm around her waist, like he might have done perhaps with her mother when he was early-married to her.

'I can afford to ask a nice price,' he said. 'I never put anything on the market that I'm ashamed to stand behind!'

Mr Mallon looked for a minute into her father's eyes, and then he looked into hers, and again like when he first rode into the yard she felt a fated weight in the moment, and knew that it wasn't altogether about the meadow grass the men were talking, either of them. It was no longer the olden times, when marriages were arranged. Now such carry-on was laughed at and mocked, but her father and Mallon were making a match for her all the same. There and then.

And she wanted it that way! Yes. Yes. And her heart was so filled with joy that when just then, high up in the blue sky, out of sight, a lark began to trill, it seemed as if it was her heart singing out for all to hear. She looked at Tod Mallon. And he looked at her.

'Well, I'm a man that's willing to pay a good price for a thing if it's true to its worth,' he said. He turned back to her father. 'But there's no hurry, I suppose,' he said, and he nodded at the grass. 'It can be let go a while longer, wouldn't you say?'

'Oh, a good while longer,' her father said, as if glad he could be prodigal with something. 'Take your time. You'll have the first refusal anyway, I promise you that!'

They shook hands then, with a strong manly clasp of their hands that dipped them forward and downward as if they were two middle-sized men, instead of the tall men they both were. Tod Mallon straightened up first.

'Good-bye, sir,' he said to her father.

'Good-bye, Miss!' he said to her. No more. The next minute he was in the trap and spanking down the road. She and her father stayed looking after him for as long as they could see the tip of his whip over the road-hedge.

'Well, that's that!' her father said then. He was in great spirits. As they moved back into the middle of the yard and met Jake coming against them he was almost gloating. 'I told you that was the best bit of meadow in the countryside.'

'Did he make an offer?' Jake asked dourly.

'No,' said her father, 'but I put out a feeler and I'm well satisfied.'

But when her father went into the cowshed Jake looked at her queerly.

'What did you think of the fine Mr Mallon? He'll be looking for more than the meadow before long, I'd say!'

'I don't know what you mean.'

Jake only sneered. 'Oh, not you!' he said.

She walked away from him and went back towards the gate leading into the meadow. Leaning over the gate she remembered the covetous look in Mr Mallon's eyes. Her own eyes seemed to see the field for the first time. Was I blind before? she thought wonderingly. Then she went after her father into the cowshed.

'Well, girl?' he said gaily, when she came up to him in the semi-darkness that was slatted with light from the loosely jointed boards.

In the weeks that followed she got on better with her father than ever before. And even poor Tom didn't seem to rub him up the wrong way either, or at least not as often as he usually did.

'What has him in such good form these days?' Tom asked her with a puzzled look on his face.

'I don't know,' she lied, but later that evening she returned to the subject. 'Tom,' she said impulsively, 'why don't you take courage while he's in good humour and tell him about you and Flossie?'

Because, cautious and all as Tom was, she knew he and Flossie Sauran were meeting oftener and oftener after dark in the evenings and on Sunday afternoons. If her father knew he'd flay him. Tom got no encouragement at all in that line. She didn't know why their father made this difference between her brother and herself, unless it was that he identified something of himself in her and not in Tom. One day, when she was in town with him, they met a cattle dealer who told her he knew her when she was only a sparkle in her father's eyes. Her father was delighted.

'She has the same sparkle in *her* eye I can tell you!' he said meaningfully.

There was very little sparkle in Tom's eye. All the same she couldn't see why he was so covert about his meetings with Flossie.

'He can't kill you, Tom!' she said. 'Why don't you

tell him! He might think the more of you for it. Tell him!'

But Tom was terrified of him.

'Take care would he hear you!' he said, looking over his shoulder nervously, although at the time their father was out in the fields counting the cattle.

'He'll have to know sometime!' she said, but lightly, because already her mind was running ahead to the time when she herself would be married. She'd have some authority over her father then, and she'd talk to him about Tom; straight talk too. And she'd ask Flossie to her house, and let her and Tom meet openly and naturally. Tod might put in a word for them, then, too.

For Tod Mallon had come again. He'd bought the meadow. And he'd called after that again to bargain for the after-grass.

'That fellow means business,' her father said, making no disguise now about his meaning. He pulled her hair affectionately. 'After-grass indeed! No beast could want for after-grass that has the sweet pickings Mallon's can get any day down between the flaggers in his own river-field. Mark my words, if he takes our after-grass, there's more in his mind than he's declared!'

As if she didn't know! The old collie in the yard knew! He had given up barking at Tod, and he a cross dog that barked at people going past the house every day of there lives.

She would of course have liked Mallon to show his hand more plainly, and to her instead of only to her father. She was unsettled. Most of the day she hung about the yard or stood at the door to see if there might be a trap coming up the road, with the tip of a whip showing over the hedge. She was happy all the same, and it was good to look out over the fields. How sweet must be the moment when feelings roused by such beauty could be shared with another soul? She was only impatient for the moment of sharing to come. And it was slow in coming.

For one thing Tod never came to the house unless he had business with her father. She would have begun to think there was nothing at all between her and him if it weren't for Jake. Since Mallon appeared on the scene Jake had got bolder because he felt that now he would be playing safe. More than ever her flirting with him was only a whiling away of the long tedious summer evenings.

But her father seemed to take a different view of things, and several times now when she and Jake met at the pump in the yard, or when Jake came to the kitchen door to get the pig-mash, she'd seen her father glaring at him. But she no more feared her father than she feared the feints of Jake because she felt wiser and more knowing than either of them. For all the fears the farmers had of their daughters getting mixed up with a labouring man, those fears were nothing to the fears the fellows themselves had of making trouble between them and the men that gave them their hire. Oh, she knew Jake! She knew him better than her father knew him.

If only her father had known, that day in the church-yard, that it was talking about Mallon she and Jake were!

She had come out from the service, and was going through the churchyard, down the grass path to the stile that led into their own fields, when she'd seen Jake standing under the old yew trees that vaulted the path. He was going back to the yard to rinse the milk cans, a job that was often left till after church on Sunday. And when he saw her he waited.

'I suppose you'll be going home the other way one of these days,' he said, and he nodded towards the path that led out to the road. And she knew Tod must have been somewhere in sight. She'd seen him in the church, but he'd left before her, and although that was why she had hurried out she hadn't seen him anywhere. She hadn't wanted to stare around too obviously. She was so glad to see Jake, because it gave her an excuse for lingering a bit, and while she was talking to him she was looking back casually over her shoulder. It wouldn't matter if Tod saw her as long as she was talking to someone. It might provoke him. Jake was only a workman, but he was a fine looking man, and young blood didn't make the same distinctions as old blood.

Jake wasn't one for hanging back though. He wanted to get his work done; he was going to a football match after his dinner.

'Are you coming?' he said.

'What's the hurry?' she said, stealing another backward glance as she spoke. Tod was still in the churchyard. He was standing at the gate talking to an old woman from a cottage near him, who did a bit of baking for him and washed his shirts. He was facing her way, but she couldn't be sure if he'd seen her or not. 'What's the hurry, Jake?' she repeated absently.

But Jake gave her arm a pull, and his voice was rough. 'I know what's in your mind,' he said. 'Be careful. You're not going to make a teaser out of me!'

She turned to laugh at him, but there was a look in his eyes that made her restless. If only she could bring that look into the eyes of the other one!

That was the moment her father came over the stile.

Her first feeling when she saw him was only simple surprise. She thought he was far away in the upland pasture putting a head-collar on a mare, to bring her down to the home-fields. What had brought him back? What had brought him here?

The next minute he raised the head-collar.

'Don't!' she screamed, when she realised why he'd swung the strap, and she saw the buckle glittering in the air. 'We were only talking, father,' she screamed.

For one instant it seemed that he had stayed the buckle in mid-air, and she saw by his eyes that her father did, in that moment, believe her. But she knew him. Her innocence would not save her. He must have glimpsed her from the fields, and thought it was with Tod Mallon she was dallying. When he'd seen it was not Mallon, but Jake, he'd been bitterly disappointed. It was for his disappointment she would suffer.

To this day, she wasn't sure if he'd missed or not with his first lash at her. She fell on the ground all right, but she could have flung herself down cowering, cowering before the blow.

'Father, father! Do you want to make a show of me before everyone?'

It was the wrong thing to say. He threw a glance beyond her to where the few people who were still standing around the church gate had drawn together astonished, not knowing what to do. And among them, rooted to the ground with astonishment, was Tod.

Then, before her father swung the headcollar again, she covered her face and chest. He would strike her now for sure. He was in the wrong, but it was she who'd put him in the wrong, and he'd strike her for it. Mortified at what he had done, and unable to undo it, he would put himself altogether beyond the comprehension of gapers and gossipers, by hitting her again.

It was the second blow did the harm. It fell on her leg and tore open the skin. Yet at the time she hadn't felt any bitterness. If anything, it was pity for her father himself that she felt, pity for the damage that, through her, he had done to his own secret vanities and ambitions. But of course, then, no one knew, neither her father, nor herself, nor Tod, nor anyone, that the cut was going to fester and fail to heal.

In the days that followed, her father must often have felt guilty. She'd caught him slyly looking at her at times, and about a week afterwards – it must have been the next Sunday – when she was getting ready to go out to church he shouted at her.

'Take off that stocking!' he said. 'Do you want to get dye into the cut and destroy yourself altogether!'

She took off the stocking. Her leg was throbbing and she wasn't sorry to stay at home that day. After a few weeks tied to the house though, it was a different matter. And one lovely evening – such a lovely evening – she decided to take a walk if it was only a little limp of a one.

Her father was in the yard when she opened the door.

'A person would think you'd want to hide your shame, instead of going out to show it off!'

Tears rushed into her eyes. How could he speak to her like that? Him who did it? How could he? She had a lot to learn. She didn't know then of all the years that lay ahead when it would have been a relief if he sneered at her instead of her having to endure the terrible silence that came down with respect to her infirmity. Not only her father's silence, but Tom's. Not only the silence of those in the house with her, but of the whole parish. No one ever spoke directly of it to her. Except Tod. He always asked about it, right from the start.

The first night, after it happened, he'd come straight up to the house to ask openly about it. Her father was out, and Tom and she were in the kitchen.

'It's Mallon!' Tom said when he saw him coming. 'You'd better not let him see you.' But she limped to the door.

'How are you?' Tod asked, and his eyes went at once to the rag she had tied around her leg. It was an old sheet torn up for the purpose.

'You saw what happened?'

'I only saw him strike you. I didn't see why he did it.'

'You saw all there was to see!' she flashed. 'I was only talking to Jake Hewett.'

He looked unbelievingly at her.

'A father would hardly strike his daughter for that!' he said, and his voice was harsh. But she was hardly going to bother to clear herself, such a feeling of joy went through her at that harsh note in his voice. Now I know he cares, she thought. But she had to say something.

'Don't you believe me?' she said.

'I don't know,' he said. 'I don't know!' And with that he turned and went away, without a word to Tom who had come out and was standing beside them like a fool while all this was going on.

'I thought he wanted to see Father?' Tom said, looking stupidly after Mallon as he drove out of the yard.

'Did you!' she cried, and she laughed. 'That's all you know!'

If it weren't for the ache in her leg she would have thought what happened was lucky and that it might be the cause of bringing things to a head. She went back to the kitchen and rolled down her stocking and looked at the cut. It might be a good thing to stoup it again, because it would want to heal quickly if she was to follow up whatever advantage she had gained.

But every time she cleaned out the cut, pus formed in it again. No matter how often she stouped it, no scab stuck to it for long enough to let it dry.

At last one day about six months after it happened, when her father and Tom were at the three-day Fair of Ballinasloe, she got Jake to drive her in to the dispensary in the town, but she didn't put much stock on what the doctor told her.

Next morning when she and her brother were alone together for a minute in the kitchen, she asked Tom a question cautiously. 'Is an ulcer a bad thing, Tom?'

Tom was sharpening the scythe up against the kitchen table, and drawing the whetstone slowly along the blade, as if it was to get music out of it.

'In a beast, is it?' he asked absently.

'Man or beast,' she said weakly.

'They say it's bad,' he said. 'Why?'

'No why!' she said dejectedly.

Tod knew all about ulcers though.

'Is that leg no better?' he asked her irritably one day when he had come on some business with her father. 'Would it be ulcerating? Did you see a doctor about it? An ulcer can get incurable if it's neglected.'

His voice was cruel, but she knew what made it cruel, and she wouldn't have had it any other way.

'You believe me now, Tod, don't you?' she said softly. 'It was only because he was a working man that my father was annoyed with me for talking to him, and – '

'I know,' he said sharply, interrupting her. 'I be-lieve you.' But there was a look on his face that made her heart go cold. It was a look she had seen once on Tom's face when they were children. He'd lost the new watch that their father had given him for his Confir-mation. He'd looked for it all day on the fringe of the meadow, and in the matted grass of the headland. Then just as they were going to go home, she heard him draw a breath like a cry, and when she ran over to where he was standing in the middle of a plank that served as a foot-bridge across a ditch, she thought he was daft, because there was the watch on the bottom of the ditch, yet he had looked as if he was going to cry.

'But you've found it, Tom!' she'd said.

'I wish I hadn't,' he said, and looking again she saw the watch was under a foot of water and she under-stood then the look on his face.

That was the look on Tod's face. He wished he didn't believe her. Now that she was useless to him.

Because, by then she knew herself that her leg was

F

never going to heal. It didn't come against her too much. She could work about the house and the inner yard, she could churn and bake, but she'd be no use for the heavier jobs of a farmer's wife, calf-rearing or pig-feeding or the like.

A fierce resentment went through her. That was country life for you! In the town it would have been different. But in the country, the only thing men thought about was breeding a family, and getting as much work out of a woman as a beast. But she regretted her bitterness when she remembered the first day Tod had driven across the cobbles, and their eyes had met. She knew she was doing him an injustice. He too would have welcomed a bit of romance in his life, only he wasn't prepared to have it at the cost of everything else.

He came less and less often to the house. Sometimes he didn't call for months, and always when he called he had a strict purpose. Now, though, instead of being glad, her father found it hard to be civil to him. The only chance she got to as much as see him was in church on Sundays. She used to sit behind him, on the other side of the aisle so she could look across slant-ways, without being seen, but he must have felt her eyes upon him, because after a time he took to standing at the back of the church. And always when the service was over he went out quickly and drove away. He had given up the trap. He was one of the first in the countryside to have a motor-car. She hated that car. It seemed to take him still further out of her life. It would keep him eligible a long time in the eyes of the giddy young girls growing up around them, in spite of his ageing appearance, and his solitary ways.

Tod was ageing fast. On the rare occasions when she met him she could see that. And her heart was stabbed with sadness for them both. But he never married – and in this her heart could still exult, and standing at the window sometimes looking into the fields, she was unable to stem the little false feelings of hope that stirred in her, above all in summer time, the time she first met him. Then, when the fields were rich and flowering, the hedges flecked with blossom, and when the scent of the clover sweetened the air, she used to argue with herself.

It ought to be enough, she'd tell herself, the beauty and the peace of it all. But it wasn't. It was meant to be shared.

And as the years wore on, and as her leg got a lot less painful and gave her less trouble, sometimes when she looked around her in the church, it seemed to her that the forced rest she had got from having to mind it had left her, in the end, a younger-looking woman than the women who were girls when she was a girl, and who were now worn out with child-bearing and the brutal work on the land.

Even Tod remarked on it one day in the town.

'You're looking well,' he said, and although it was a mild enough remark, she knew it meant she must be looking well indeed.

'I'm feeling well!' she said. And she laughed recklessly. 'I was thinking only the other Sunday that I'm wearing better than a lot of my neighbours.'

It was a flash of her old boldness, a boldness that had gone utterly from her spirit much less her tongue. But Tod turned aside abruptly.

'They had their strength when they needed it,' he

said. Somehow she didn't feel humiliated or hurt. It showed he still cared, and it came into her mind that if she really knew – for certain – not just by hints and insinuations, but *for certain*, that he had loved her, and that that was why he never married – and never would – she would have been satisfied. He'd be hers in a kind of way then at least.

It might be too small a thing to satisfy most women, but it would satisfy her – or so she thought. But would she be able to keep such knowledge a secret? she wondered. If she didn't tell someone, just one person, wouldn't the truth be little better than her dreamings and imaginings? But who could she tell? Flossie Sauren was the only one who might come near to understanding.

Poor Flossie! She and Tom had never married either, so although Flossie and herself didn't meet often there was a bond between them. Not that she had much sympathy for Flossie, for it seemed to her that whereas she and Tod had been kept apart by inmost, unknowable causes hidden in the human heart – Tom and Flossie were unmarried only because they hadn't any spirit.

One evening she tried to goad Tom into doing something about Flossie even at that late date. It was again the eve of the Three Day Fair in Ballinasloe, and for the first time in their lives their father was not going. Tom was going on his own. He was in the kitchen blacking his shoes.

'He mustn't be feeling well if he's not going, Tom,' she said. 'Will you manage by yourself?' He would be buying springers, a knacky job.

When Tom didn't answer she saw how stupid

she'd been. He was glad to be going alone. He looked younger and livelier than he'd done for a long time. He was excited too, almost queerly excited.

'You'd think you were going to a wedding,' she said.

She didn't often make jokes, but the look he gave her that evening cured her for good.

'What made you say that?' He stopped in the middle of blacking the shoe in his hand.

'Tom! Don't look at me like that!' she said. 'I was only thinking how well you looked. And anyway, I don't see what harm it was! By rights it ought to be a wedding – your own!' She ran over to him. 'Oh Tom, I'm not standing in your way, am I? You know what I mean! If you're waiting for me to be gone out of here and the way clear for you to take in a wife, then you'll never marry. Because I'll never be gone. It's not my fault! You know that, don't you, Tom? But I wouldn't be in anyone's way. You can tell Flossie I'd be good to her. I would. I promise you!'

He'd started blacking the other shoe while she was saying this, but he left down the blacking brush and taking his foot off the chair he went to the window and pointed out towards the yard where their father could be seen clattering across the cobbles with the yard lamp, seeing everything was in order.

'What life would a woman have in this house with him?' Tom asked.

It was true.

'Here, let me do those shoes for you,' she said, in amendment for her insensitivity.

'They're done enough,' he said.

They were shining like laurel leaves. She couldn't help exclaiming.

'Aren't they very light-soled shoes for wearing to the Fair?'

But oh how touchy he was! She could have bitten out her tongue for noticing them.

'I want something besides hob-nail boots to wear in the evenings in the lodging-house parlour, don't I?' he said.

'That's right, Tom,' she said weakly, thinking that when his father went with him it must have been very little Tom saw of the parlour. No doubt he'd always been sent off to bed like a gossoon, to be up at the first screech of daylight.

He'd be a new man if he was his own master, she thought. And, where she would have felt guilty thinking of gain to herself if anything happened to their father, it seemed different altogether to think of the gain to Tom.

How long will it be till he gets the place, she wondered? It seemed that their life would go on, day after day, for ever, as it had always done, until it was less of a duration than a kind of immediate successiveness: a kind of eternity.

'Ah well, he'll enjoy the Fair anyway,' she thought. And next morning she felt happy for him as she watched him go off in the dawn. Maybe he'd have things to tell her when he came back.

She tried to imagine the lodging-house parlour. Would there be young women there, playing the piano to amuse the farmers and the dealers? It would be hard on poor Flossie if Tom were to put his eye on some young one, but somehow she couldn't think of him making advances to any woman, but only sitting down, pleased with being away from home, and proud of his shoes, shining like laurel leaves.

The whole three days of the Fair he was in her mind continually and she tried hard not to be impatient for his return. Their father too was looking forward to his return home. The Fair seemed to have gained in importance for their father by his being unable to go to it. He never quit reading the newspaper, noting the weights of the beasts, and the prices they were making.

'I ought to have gone, no matter how I felt,' he said. 'He'll buy backward springers: that's what he'll do. He has no experience.'

Tom didn't buy backward springers. He bought none.

'They were going too dear,' he said, and she thought at the time he said it lamely.

'You didn't buy any beast at all?' she echoed.

She was nearly speechless with surprise.

Their father wasn't speechless though: far from it.

'Is it pay for four days' food and lodgings and nothing to show for it?' he shouted. 'God damn it, what kind of a fool are you?' He looked as if he might strike him. Then he sat down heavily on a chair behind him.

'Are you all right, father?' she cried. 'Tom! Tom! There's something the matter with him! Quick! – hold him.'

There was something wrong. They got him to bed and sent for the doctor. He'd had a stroke.

She forgot about Tom and Flossie for a long time after that.

In seven years from that day their father never left the bed. When she did occasionally think about Tom and Flossie she didn't like to mention the matter again. It was linked in her mind with her unfortunate joke on the eve of the Fair. And when once, after many years, she did mention it, Tom cut her short.

'I've had enough of that!' he said crossly.

She felt he too was thinking of the night before the Fair, and he didn't want to be reminded of what she'd said. But a few minutes later he spoke of that night himself.

'I killed him!' he said.

'Nonsense,' she said. 'Anyway, he's far from dead,' she added.

Their father was not far from death though. It was the very next day he asked about her leg. And the day after that he was dead.

When their father was laid out and she sat beside the bed, she found herself pondering on the changes that would come. Already the house was filling with people. One by one the neighbours had congregated. It was almost like the way, one by one, cattle are drawn over to a part of a field where something unusual has happened, where a tree has fallen, or where one of themselves has been lamed and is unable to rise.

At first the voices were subdued, but as the house filled up, and the neighbouring women saw small things to be done, and set about doing them, there was more live air about the house than there had been for years. If there ever had!

It was like a breaking of ice. And as when the ice of winter is breaking, and the growth of spring is seen to have already started underneath, she felt within her a great expectancy. But expectancy of what? She didn't know. She did wonder, though, if Tod would come to the funeral.

He didn't come. He was the only one for miles around who stayed away from both the house and the cemetery.

'A nice neighbour, that fellow!' Tom said, when all was over and he and she were alone on the day after the burial.

'He never forgave father,' she said.

Tom stood up abruptly. He was still in his best clothes, but he was restless, and didn't seem to have much fancy for sitting talking. Above all, he didn't seem to like the turn the talk had taken.

'I think I'll change my clothes,' he said.

She knew what that meant. He was going out with the old scythe to cut weeds. He's married to that old scythe, she thought, partly bitter, partly amused. And a few minutes later, when she heard steps in the yard, she thought it was him coming back for something he'd forgotten: the whetstone, or the wrench.

But it was Tod.

'You didn't come to the funeral,' she said, for the sake of saying something. She didn't ask him in, but went out to him, and they both walked across the yard towards the gate leading into the meadow. It was summer time again.

'I never forgave him,' he said, leaning over the gate and looking down into the deep grass.

They were the words she had used only a moment before to Tom.

'For what he did to me?' she asked softly.

He looked straight at her face.

' – and to me,' he said.

Like a lark in the sky – like when she was young – her heart sang out for joy. But under a hedge of the field in front of them, a corncrake made himself heard with a harsh sound, not like a song at all, more like the sound of the clappers at Tenebrae.

'He came between us: he spoiled everything for us.'

It was true, she thought. At last – at last – after all these years it was said. Not in the words of youth. Not in the way she would once have wanted to hear it – but in the only way it could be said now. She looked at him with pity.

He saw the look in her eyes, and he took a step nearer to her, but she moved back. Long ago she had condemned him for not knowing that love was enough, and for thinking only of breeding a family. Now, when the days of her fertility were over, she saw things in another light. Her heart was flooded with the old familiar feeling of hope in the future, but she realised at last that it wasn't from Tod any more that she looked for hope's fulfilment. It was too late. In the intensity of this realisation her mind fastened urgently on her brother. Tom! He was younger than her. And Flossie was younger still. There was time yet surely for them to be fruitful if they married!

I must talk to Tom again, she thought. It was no longer a vague romantic notion that animated her mind. Nor was it Flossie and Tom's satisfaction either that she looked for from their union. It isn't us that matter any more, she thought, Tod or me, or Tom or Flossie. It's those who come after us.

Looking past Tod, she let her eyes fill with the

beauty of the field he had once bid for, the field that was again heavy with meadow. Oh, to stand leaning over that gate with a crowd of youngsters around her – or even one small creature, gripping her hand – Oh, the joy of that!

Impatiently, she put out her hand.

'Thank you for coming, Tod,' she said, but when he looked as if he were going to say something else, she gathered her arms to her breast. 'I have to see Tom about something. I was going down to him when you came.'

He had to stand aside to let her pass, and when she did, he must have seen there was nothing for him to do but to go back out to where he had left his car on the road. Once she looked back at him, and she saw he was standing by the door of the car looking after her. She too stood for a minute looking at him, but it was taking leave of him she was, in that last backward look. Then she hurried on downward to the river.

Tom and Flossie would have to be married at once. At once. They mustn't be let wait any longer, not even in decency to the dead.

'Tom! Tom!' she called out as she drew near him. Already she had forgotten Tod Mallon. He was unimportant to her at last. 'I couldn't stay in the house, Tom,' she cried when she reached him. 'I had to come down to you. I know you hated talking about it the last time, but it's different now, isn't it?' She hesitated, but only for a minute. ' – About you and Flossie, I mean?'

He had stopped scything when she first spoke, but when he took in her words, he assumed the stiffness of a stranger. Then deliberately, and without answering her, he began again to pull the scythe heavily through the reeds.

She tried to take his silence for attentiveness.

'You'll have to wait a little while, I know that,' she said apologetically, 'but we could have everything planned.' Her excitement rushed back and overwhelmed her. She didn't notice the pronoun she had used. 'We could talk it over with Flossie, and begin to get things ready for the wedding without anybody knowing. With me in the know she could come up here, and she and I could both be getting the house in order. We could – '

Tom stopped scything again, but he took up the whetstone and drew it across the blade. Then he looked coldly at her.

'Take it easy,' he said. 'Take it easy, will you!'

'Oh, but Tom! How can you say that? After all the years that have been wasted. Time is so precious now – for both of you.'

But her eagerness seemed to annoy him.

'Didn't you hear me telling you to take it easy!' he said. 'For God's sake! Death always brings changes, but there's no hurry. There is *no hurry*, I tell you,' he repeated, and this time he said it so positively and so meaningfully she felt perhaps there was more to him, that he was perhaps deeper than she had ever known.

'It wouldn't be the same as long ago,' she said less confidently, 'but surely it would be – '

'Better than nothing? Is that what you mean?' His voice was so bitter she began to get frightened.

'No,' she said standing firm all the same, 'that's not what I mean. But wouldn't you like to have a family growing up around you, Tom? Wouldn't any man?'

When he seemed to ponder this thought for a moment, her hopes rose, but the next minute he looked her full in the face with a strange expression.

'I'll have no family,' he said shortly. 'I can tell you that now.'

'How do you know?' she cried. 'You never can tell. I – '

He put out his hand then and caught her by the arm, and his grip was so fierce she nearly fainted.

'How do I know? How does any man know? My father thought I was a gom. I put up with that, but I didn't know you took me for one too? I may have been afraid of him – afraid to face up to him openly – but that didn't say I let him own me body and soul. When I said we'd have no family I meant what I said. Don't look so stupid! You know what I mean!' She didn't, but as she struggled to understand he sneered. 'Oh, it's not what you think now either,' he said. 'It was all respectable and as it ought to be, or as near as we could make it to what it ought to be. We're properly married and all that, but it's not the great cause for rejoicing that you seem to think it. Not in the way you mean anyway. If we were going to have a child we'd have had one long ago.'

She stared at him as if he was a stranger. She said nothing for a minute. She was only beginning to understand. If they'd had a child he'd have had to tell his father, she thought, and he was glad he hadn't had to face up to it.

They were standing near an old thorn tree, and she sank back against it weakly. She was utterly confounded by what he had told her. Looking at him, she could see he felt bad for her. He probably didn't know what injury he had done her, but she could see he wanted to make amends.

'I was going to tell you a couple of times,' he said, 'but I thought it was safer for your own sake not to be wise to it. And then as the years went by – '

She looked up quickly. 'Years? How many years?'

'Oh, I don't know,' he said indifferently. Then he made an effort. 'Before father got ill of course! Nine or ten years I'd say, and about six or seven since we got married. As a matter of fact I thought you had got wind of our plans the night before the wedding. It was the night I was supposed to be going to Ballinasloe to the Fair.' Suddenly he put his hand up to his forehead in a mild distress. 'You remember when I came back I told him I didn't buy the springers – and he flew into a rage – it brought on that first stroke he got. I used to think for a long time that it was my fault he was stricken. Because I wasn't at the Fair at all. I didn't go near Ballinasloe. Flossie met me in the town and we went up to Dublin and got married.'

It all came back to her. The thin shoes she thought he was polishing for the lodging-house parlour! She'd thought him odd that night: she remembered it well. So that was what he'd been up to! She looked at him. She never thought he would have had it in him.

Seeing the surprise on her face her brother may have felt a momentary flash of the liveliness and spirit that had led to his one solitary escapade, but no doubt it died away, at the thought of the long unproductive years that were ushered in by that brief bravado.

'Well, that's the way things are,' he said matter-of-factly. 'You see what I mean when I say there's no hurry. There'll have to be changes, I realise that – but

I don't know yet what they'll be. I doubt if Flossie will want to come to live here in the fields now, being used for so long to living near the road. It's lonely in there, you know. I might go down and live in her place if her sister went to Dublin, and there's some talk of that. It might work out. Their place is small, but we'll have no use for a big place.' He looked at her suddenly and he looked tired and helpless. 'There's you to consider, too, of course. It'd be very lonely for you here on your own. I suppose you might find some place in Dublin too and then we could sell this place. But as I said, there's no hurry. And now, will you leave me alone for God's sake and let me get on with the scything. You know it's the only bit of pleasure I get.'

There was no choice for her but to turn and make her way back to the house. Evening was coming down quickly, and the western sky glowed with so fierce a light that as the homing rooks flew across the flaming path of the burning sun, they became transparent as glass birds.

Reaching the door of the house she stood and looked back. The light of day had not yet faded, but a few stars had made their way through the heavens. Their beauty stabbed her through and through. She used to want to share that beauty, first with Tod, and then, in a last hysterical longing, she'd wanted to share it with anyone – anyone – even the unborn. But now there would be no one with whom to share it, ever. Why did she have this terrible need? We try to make nature a part of our life, she thought, and what are we but a part of it?

She looked down towards the river-field. It was almost too dark to see Tom, and it must have been too dark for him to see what he was doing, but he was still swinging the scythe expertly from side to side, slicing through the reeds and the wild grasses, with a gesture so true and natural it might have been a branch swaying in the wind.

Villa Violetta

Before she was awarded a Fellowship herself it seemed to Vera that everyone on a grant went to Florence. She had been there with Richard and she wanted his children to see it. After his death, looking back it seemed that the stones of Florence that had given added warmth to the sunlight, had also given increase to their happiness.

She did not realise that, without him, everything would be different. She had had no warning that Florence would appear in no better light than any other city in which a young widow arrived alone with three small children, very little of the language, and no grasp at all of the currency. Tired and hungry, she had to leave the children sitting on the suitcase on the platform while she went to change money, having forgotten to do it at Victoria Station. Then, when she'd given them something to eat in the station café, she had to drag them with her to look for somewhere to stay the night, not having made an advance booking either. Within minutes of her arrival in Florence her incompetence was brought fully home to her. In the end she had to take a hotel at random and near the station at that – a notoriously expensive area in any city. The tariff at the Hotel Puccini was terrifying. The thought of paying so much for one night gave her a sinking feeling as if, already, a broadside had been fired into her budget.

Yet a week later they were still in the Puccini. And it didn't matter how well two of the children behaved at any one time, there was always a third who spoiled everything, creating rows and arguments. Her little girls, between the three of them, made it impossible for her to hunt around for reasonably priced accommodation. As for finding a school for them – that she had to postpone indefinitely. Finding a school should, of course, have been her first concern, but after a week in the Puccini with them her nerves were so fretted she had only one thought and that was to get into a flat of her own where she could let them run around without fear of their wrecking the place.

In fairness to the children, though, it was she herself who did what damage was done. It was she who tilted the stupid little lampshade over the bed, and burned a hole in it. It was she who was responsible for the exploding of a bottle of Lacrimae Christi, by leaving it – corked – on a radiator! On that occasion, however, the management could not have been kinder.

'*Parfumo! Parfumo!*' the young manager cried with delight, as he summoned a waiter to mop up the carpet.

It was not until she got her bill at the end of the week that Vera really began to panic. At this rate her money would be gone in a month. That was an exaggeration, of course, but it showed how frantic she had become.

At the end of a second week, when they were still in the Puccini, she was nearly at breaking-point. She had completely lost her head. Now, every lira she spent might as well have been her last. Yet they were still eating all their meals in the hotel because it meant she could put Linda to bed at a reasonable hour and by paying a small supplement have a simple supper sent up to the child's room. Evening meals out in a trattoria had proved disastrous. It might have helped if she had moved into a cheaper hotel, but she was so bad at managing money she shrank from the incidental expenses of a temporary move – the taxis, and the tipping. It seemed cheaper, in the long run, to stay where she was until the move would be permanent.

The daily dribbling away of small sums of money upset her out of all proportion to their total. She'd never become sufficiently settled in her mind to master the values of the Italian currency. The children – even Linda – understood the foreign monies better than her. In a crisis they'd dive into her bag and pull up fistfuls of small change which they handed out with the accuracy of a coin-dispenser. At least in the Puccini she could have everything put down on the bill, and have a record she could check, and, if necessary, dispute. At heart, though, she sometimes thought her real reason for staying on at the hotel was that it had become for her what the Duomo was for other visitors: a landmark. It was the only place to which and from which she could make her way without getting lost. The maps of the city that she got from the Italian tourist office were no use. According to them, Florence was made up of the Arno, its bridges, gardens, galleries, palaces, and famous churches. The maps were really nothing more than beautiful posters, all green and gold and azure. They did not include the suburbs, and it was there apparently the cheaper apartment-houses were to be found. To get to these she had to travel by trolley buses, with doors like a guillotine that at any minute might slice one of the children in two. As well as that the trolleys were so jammed with people she usually got carried several blocks too far.

At the end of the third week she had called so often at the tourist office that Carlotta, the young lady in charge, was in despair about them. Time and again, with Linda perched on top of the counter, the young lady would spread out the map, twisting it this way and that, trying to teach Vera how to find her way in the maze of little streets. If only – Carlotta said – she would try to make the Duomo her point of reference instead of the Puccini. Then, generously distributing more coloured brochures to the children – although by now she must have known Vera was letting Linda cut them up and paste them into her scrapbook – she'd come out into the street to make sure they at least started out in the right direction. To no avail! Before they'd have crossed the first piazza Vera would have lost her way again. Almost crying, she'd open the map and start twisting it around again as if it was a turntable that of itself would set her right.

One afternoon when she was standing in the street turning the map round and round, a smart red sports car drew up to the curb beside her.

'Lost again?' a voice asked. 'Can I help?'

It was Carlotta. It was her free afternoon, she explained, adding that, as she had spent a year in Cambridge, it was her pleasure to help English-speaking visitors. 'Why don't you permit me to drive you around to look at some of those places?' she asked, referring to the latest list of officially recommended accommodation she had given them. Vera's hand went frantically into her pocket. Had she lost the list?

'Oh, no matter!' Carlotta smiled understandingly. 'I know it by heart. Allow me!' she said, throwing open the door of the car. The children piled into the back, and gratefully Vera sank into the seat beside her. 'Now, which shall we try first?' said Carlotta. 'The Pensione Appenina, the Pensione Hadrian, or the Pensione Bougainvillea? They are all near here. This is a very good area for pensione.'

Was I blind? Vera wondered. There were pensione in every street, and in every piazza, and in some places there were little galaxies of them clustered together. But did she want a pensione? She found it hard to rid herself of the insular idea they were only glorified lodging-houses.

'I had thought an apartment would be best,' she said feebly, when Carlotta drew up outside Pensione Appenina.

To Carlotta an apartment seemed quite out of the question.

'You'd never get any work done, unless you got a servant and – ' the girl shook her head, ' – servants are no longer cheap in Italy. And they are very quick to size up their employers – I feel sure that they'd *play* on you – terribly.'

Vera shuddered. A new fear on top of the rest! Meekly she stepped out on to the pavement, and they all followed Carlotta into the pensione.

'What a beautiful room!' Vera cried, when a small self-effacing woman in black bowed them into a large room on the ground floor. It looked out on the Arno from two large windows draped with heavy tapestry curtains. Surreptitiously Vera fingered the curtains. They looked hand-embroidered. 'Careful, Linda,' she called out, because the child had climbed up on a window sill and was trying to open the window. Gloria and Bea were entranced.

'Are we sleeping here tonight?' they asked loudly.

Discreetly Carlotta drew attention away from them by quickly addressing the woman.

'We will telephone, if the Signora decides to take the room,' she said in English. The woman bowed graciously in acknowledgment of this courtesy.

'Isn't there a chance it might be gone?' Vera whispered, but Carlotta shook her head. Vera was still worried. 'We could leave a deposit – ' she suggested – 'a small deposit but – '

'You mustn't take the first room you see!' Carlotta admonished.

When a few minutes later Vera saw the Pensione Bougainvillea she realised how right Carlotta was. The Bougainvillea was even nicer than the Appenina.

'I'd no idea they'd be so nice!' she exclaimed. 'The furniture is exquisite.'

'It's been in the same family for generations,' Carlotta whispered. 'A very old Florentine family. It is the Contessa herself who is showing us the rooms.'

Vera blushed for not having known.

'That is partly why the rooms are so expensive,' Carlotta explained, and opening her handbag she consulted a list. 'Actually there's very little difference between this and the Appenina if you like this better.' Calmly, then, she announced the rent.

'Oh, but that's almost as much as I'm paying in the hotel!' Vera cried.

Carlotta's dismay, which was instantly seen, was not for Vera's ignorance, however, but for her own. Obviously it had never occurred to her that anyone, even a foreigner, could be unaware that these specially-listed pensione would be at least as expensive as a hotel by the station.

'Some of the better-class pensione are as dear as the best hotels,' she said sharply, and she glanced involuntarily at Vera's ready-made suit. 'I did not know that money mattered,' she murmured. Then quickly, apologetically, she explained this last remark. 'I thought your government was paying!'

'It is!' Vera said. 'That's the whole point. They can't be expected to pay exorbitant rents!' She was embarrassed though, and now she in her turn glanced at Carlotta's suit. The suit was not just neat, it was chic. And of course that sports car – she was abashed. 'I've wasted a lot of your time, I'm afraid,' she said.

'Not at all!' Carlotta was trying to be polite. 'All the same we'd better go across to the other side of the Arno,' she said, piling them into the car again, and setting off very fast. In a few minutes they drew up outside yet another pensione. This one however had the air of dingy respectability Vera associated with boarding-houses at home, except that its dimensions were palatial. Indeed she heard Carlotta tell the children it had once been a de Medici palace. And as they tramped up the huge marble staircase Vera could see that the architecture was magnificent.

'Mind you don't fall, Linda,' she called out as Linda ran ahead of them up the great staircase.

On the second floor Carlotta pulled on a hand-tooled leather bell-pull. And this time when a large woman appeared Vera could have sworn she too was a Contessa. At least she was like a Contessa in an opera. Carlotta and the woman conferred together in Italian. Apparently there was only one room available, and again, the view was superb.

'The view is mentioned in our brochure,' Carlotta pointed out to Vera who, as discreetly as she could, was trying to see what the beds were like. In appearance they were regal. The one that would be hers had a carved and gilded headboard in the shape of a swan, and again the coverlet was a genuine old tapestry. But the mattress sagged dreadfully. Carlotta exchanged a few more words with the 'Contessa', then she turned to Vera, 'The rent here is less than half what it is on the other side,' she herself seemed amazed at this, and pencilled a note on her list.

'Can we think it over?' Vera asked.

Carlotta frowned. 'It's not wise to hesitate about places on this side of the Arno,' she said. 'At a rent like this it could be snapped up the moment we turn our backs.'

'Perhaps if we offered to leave a deposit – ?' Vera suggested again.

Carlotta lowered her voice. 'She'd expect at least a month's rent, I assure you. It's not at all like on the other side – over here they are *sharks*!' As she emphasised the last word Carlotta smiled. She was proud of her command of English colloquialisms. And well she might be! She had made Vera's blood freeze.

Seeing that Vera was already shepherding the children to the door, Carlotta, after another round of rapid-fire Italian with the 'Contessa' followed her out onto the landing.

'Careful, children!' Vera screamed, unnecessarily loud. 'Take Linda's hand, Gloria!' she yelled. She was filled with terror as they cascaded down the marble steps that, though dirty, looked like blocks of ice. Yet, it was she herself who nearly fell. The steps were so uneven, the centres worn into runnels.

After seeing two more pensione, both less attractive than those on the other side of the river – but both much cheaper – Vera's spirits sank.

'Are all the staircases in Florence made of marble?' she asked peevishly.

'I beg your pardon?' In spite of her Cambridge-acquired English, Carlotta was baffled.

'Mother gets upset very easily,' Gloria explained. 'Don't you, Mother?' she said comfortingly, and she linked her arm in Vera's.

Carlotta, looking as if she didn't need to be told *that*, put them into the car again. 'There's just one other place we ought to try,' she said, in a voice that made Vera feel this time she'd been given very little to say in the matter. So, when they were shown into the next pensione she hardly bothered to look at it because she was gathering all her energy to resist Carlotta. But she neglected to keep the necessary eye on Linda and the next thing she heard was the Italian girl giving the child a sharp reprimand, before turning crossly to Vera herself. 'Mrs Traske – please explain to them they must not *touch* things!'

Vera felt like giving the back-answer her children sometimes gave her. Tell them yourself. But she restrained herself and, anyway, at that moment she had to fling herself across the room to save a large porcelain urn from being knocked over. Hideous, she thought, as she steadied it. Hideous and useless! What would her life be like in one of these mausoleums? All her time would go protecting this junk.

She put her arm around Linda. 'They're tired,' she explained to Carlotta. 'And do you blame them?' she added. She glanced at the girl's hand. Easily seen she was not married! Not even engaged! In Italy at her age – what was it, twenty-four, twenty-five? – she was already an old maid. You could see she had no interest in children. It evidently wasn't true all Italians were mad about children, although – and here Vera's heart grew warm for a moment – she had to admit the waiters in the Puccini were marvellous and put up with a lot. Perhaps after all a hotel wasn't the worst place for them? For one thing, there was no need to feel under a compliment for breakages, they were put on the bill.

'Why don't we just try for a cheaper hotel than the Puccini?' she whispered to Carlotta. It was surprising a whisper could sound so aggressive.

Carlotta replied coldly. 'Hotels in Florence don't like residents. And cheap hotels simply won't take them. I can't say I blame them. They lose in the end: less tips for the staff, and that sort of thing.' She was getting very irritable. 'You really must make up your mind. All this indecision must be so bad for your children.' She swung around and spoke rapidly to the patrone, and bad and all as Vera's Italian was, she knew by the tone of Carlotta's voice she was saying something disparaging about her. Then Carlotta turned back to her. 'This is really the best you'll get for the money.'

The cheek of her. Once more Vera was about to give her the kind of answer she deserved, when to her dismay she saw Gloria advancing on Carlotta with fire in her eyes.

'Gloria, dear! Carlotta is only trying to help,' she said quickly, trying to flash a warning signal with her eyes. Was there *no* age at which a child would not find some way of being a nuisance? A row between Gloria and Carlotta at this point would put her in a worse light than ever.

She thought she had thwarted Gloria until the child whispered to her.

'I don't like her any more,' she whispered, and she looked to Bea for support. 'Neither does Bea.'

'That's not true, is it, Bea?' Vera asked unwisely, forgetting that these two older ones had only one thing in common, and that was mutual loyalty in the face of a third person; any third person: even their mother.

'I hate her!' Bea whispered.

Fortunately Carlotta hadn't heard. Unfortunately Linda had. She put her arms around the Italian girl's neck. 'Don't mind them, Carlotta, I like you!'

Unfairly Vera felt like slapping Linda. The others she felt like applauding. Carlotta had become one more force with which she had to contend. Far from being a spar to which they might cling, she was now a dead weight pulling them down.

'From the start it was a mistake to come abroad,' Vera said wildly.

Gloria and Bea at once threw their arms around her. Carlotta disengaged herself from Linda.

'What will I tell this woman?' This time she really rapped out the words, and startled, Linda ran back to her mother.

With her girls linked to her, Vera felt more able to deal with Carlotta. 'Tell her what you told the others,' she said flippantly. 'Tell her we'll think it over.'

'This room will almost certainly be gone!' Carlotta threatened. 'I think at the very least you should leave a deposit.'

'And forfeit my money. No thank you!' Vera snapped.

Carlotta looked daggers at her. Then she addressed herself to Gloria. 'Your mother will be making a great mistake if she lets this room go. Shall I say that she will telephone as soon as she gets back to the hotel?'

Gloria and Bea only giggled. They both knew that the telephone was their mother's biggest bugbear. They'd been several days in Florence before she'd found out she had to have a *gettone* for the telephone instead of coins. She'd thought all the telephones were out of order. Then, in a café, when an Englishman contemptuously handed her a *gettone* – put it into the slot for her, in fact – she'd thought it was just another coin, one that was perhaps scarce, because people hung on to it for telephoning.

'Mother's no good on the phone – ' Gloria said at last, primly.

'Well, she'll just have to get good at it,' Carlotta said dryly. 'I can't spend much more time with you. I have an appointment at five.' She turned back to the patrone to whom she spoke in Italian. That was another thing that was driving Vera mad, that the children were so much better at Italian than she was, although for six months before they left Dublin she had paid a young Italian painter to give her lessons in conversation. His name was Giuseppe, but the children always giggled when she spoke of him. 'You can't even pronounce his name, Mother,' Gloria said, partly amused, partly contemptuous. And she and Bea began to call him Joseppi. 'Well, it's Joseph in English,' she'd said, trying to justify herself. But she gave up the lessons.

And anyway no sooner had they crossed the border at Ventimiglia than every scrap of Italian deserted her, whereas the children no sooner heard it spoken than they began to pick it up. Every nuance registered with them and they gave it back true as a note of music. From the beginning they seemed to understand all that was said, and within minutes they were able to say '*Prego*' and '*Grazie*'. In a few days they were chattering freely, and her own efforts made them wince.

'Please, mother,' they'd implore. 'What is it you're trying to say?' At other times they'd giggle and start to parody her efforts, or look at each other and say 'Joseppi' before collapsing in fits of laughter.

It was with mixed feelings therefore she now saw that whatever the patrone was saying to Carlotta was double-dutch even to the children.

'What is she saying?' she asked Carlotta, nodding irritably at the landlady.

'She is saying,' Carlotta replied coldly, 'that she is surprised you don't mind subjecting your children to hotel-life.'

'It has its advantages,' Vera said tightly. Carlotta raised her eyebrows. Vera felt cornered. 'Well, the other night Linda was coughing and the night por-ter –'

Carlotta looked pityingly at her. 'Those services will all be extras on your bill, you know.'

They were now like two snipers taking pot shots at each other from opposite rooftops. And sensing something wrong Linda gave a loud wail.

'I want to go home!' she wailed.

Like the piston of the Rome express that had brought them there, a piston in Vera's mind began to beat out a message – *shouldn't have come – shouldn't have come – shouldn't have come –*.

But Gloria caught her by the arm and shook her. 'Linda only means back to the hotel, Mother, not back to Dublin.' She looked troubled, though. 'If only you'd stop thinking of yourself all the time, Mother.'

Vera couldn't believe her ears.

' – Thinking of myself? It's of you children I'm thinking – all the time.'

Gloria shrugged her shoulders. 'It comes to the same thing in the end,' she said. Then, as if she were about to take over altogether, she turned to Carlotta. 'What do other people do? We've met lots of families who were coming to Italy, and some of them had four or five children – ?'

'In almost all cases I've known,' Carlotta said evenly, 'the father came on ahead to make the practical arrangements, or if they were Americans, the wife came, but in that case the father was looking after the children.'

Vera remembered how once, when someone asked why she had not remarried, Gloria had answered for her.

'It's a wife Mother needs, not a husband!'

And at that moment Carlotta seemed to have had a momentary return of sympathy for her. She laid her gloved hand on her arm.

'With us in Italy things are easier,' she said. 'The Fellowships go to men, except in cases – ' She paused.

'Of freaks like me? Is that what you mean?' Vera was so upset now, the blood was pounding in her temples. Like a small tiger Bea sprang forward.

'You leave my mother alone!' she cried.

Vera stared. Her little girls! Did they feel so deeply for her? Why? Were they frightened? Did they think she was going to pieces?

'Bea!' she cried, but Bea was ripping into poor Carlotta.

'Can't you see my mother is tired?' she said. 'She must go back to the hotel at once.' On the last word she stamped her foot. The funny thing was that it brought Carlotta to heel.

'I am afraid I have not been of much service to you,' she said apologetically. But in a level voice, and with an extraordinarily level smile for a child, Gloria intervened.

'Don't worry,' she said. 'We'll manage.'

Vera looked gratefully at her daughters, and the four of them moved towards the door leaving Carlotta to conclude the farewell formalities with the landlady.

The girl did not join them until they were in the street. It appeared that she had something to do even before five o'clock.

'I forgot that I have to call at an employment agency,' she said coldly to Vera. 'My fiancé's receptionist is sick and I have to – '

Vera looked at her in astonishment. Her fiancé? So she was engaged! Irrationally, instead of lessening, her irritation increased. What kind of a fist would this cold creature make of children? So fussy and impatient. She glanced at Gloria, and made a sign which Gloria understood at once. Years before she had taken the two older children to a film called *The Inn of the Sixth Happiness*. It told the story of Gladys Aylward leading a group of Chinese children over a mountain during the Sino-Japanese war. All through the film Vera had cried, stealthily wiping her tears away with her fingers so the girls would not see, but when the film was over, and they came out into the lighted foyer, Gloria saw the tear-marks on her cheeks.

'Cheer up, Mother,' she said. 'You have only three children to get over the mountain.'

Well, she'd like to see what Carlotta would have made of the job. But Carlotta was volunteering further information.

'My fiancé is a doctor, but he's hopeless at practical affairs. His receptionist is sick, and I have to find him a substitute – '

Vera looked unsympathetically at her, but Carlotta was smiling complacently. 'Men!' she said. 'They're like children.'

They had reached the street now, and clearly Carlotta was eager to be rid of them, but all the same she politely motioned them towards the car. 'I'll lead you back to your hotel, of course!'

Once again Gloria intervened.

'That's not necessary, is it, Mother?' she said.

Vera did not want to let Gloria down, but she looked around her uneasily. In the distance she saw a green cupola. Was that the Duomo? Florence was so full of cupolas! They might not be able to find their way back.

'You'd be involved in a lot of one-way streets!' Carlotta warned.

'Not on foot!' Vera snapped.

It was a paltry victory, but Vera saw her children were applauding her with their eyes.

Carlotta had got into her car. 'There is one other place I forgot,' she said. 'I've never inspected it myself, but I know our office has given the address to people – when accommodation was scarce.' She seemed contrite and genuinely trying to help again. 'I've often passed it – in the car,' she said, 'and there are always one or two coaches outside the door. It seems to be very popular with tourists. That kind of person is always careful to get value for his money. The place is run by some order of nuns – Franciscans, I think.'

That kind of person!

'Your English is really excellent,' Vera said, but the sarcasm was lost on Carlotta who'd opened her elegant handbag and pulled out a card on which she scribbled an address.

'I should have thought of this place earlier,' she said, 'and then I could have driven you there.' She handed out the card, and disengaged the clutch. 'The Villa Violetta,' she said. 'That's the name.'

'Oh Mother – why did you do *that*?' Bea cried, when, after Carlotta had driven away, Vera tore up the card and threw it into a litter-bin. 'It was such a pretty name – Villa Violetta.'

'I don't like the sound of it,' Vera said irritably, and indeed untruthfully.

Some time later she turned on Bea again.

'See what you've done!' she cried, because Linda was skipping along ahead chanting the name sing-song.

'Vil-la Vio-let-ta, Vil-la Vio-let-ta!'

H

They were turning into the small court in front of the Puccini. 'It's not very nice for the hotel to find out we are thinking of moving – especially when they've been so good to us.'

The porter indeed had come to meet Linda, opening out his arms to her, and when, screeching with joy, Linda jumped into them, he carried her into the lobby in the crook of his arm. The lift-boy too jumped up from his seat, and flung open the lift doors. But most heart-warming of all, the young manager, who was really very young, came forth from his office, and waving aside the lift-boy stepped into the golden cage to conduct them upstairs himself. There was such a feeling of home-coming about their return that Vera wanted to cry – with relief this time.

Why had she felt such urgency to get out of this nice hotel? Indeed, why should they leave it at all? She need only pull herself together and find someone to stand in for her a few hours in the mornings. The hotel staff might even know of someone? As for the money – at worst she might have to curtail her stay in Italy. Who would really care about that? Not the Foundation certainly: it was what one got out of one's travels that mattered – not the duration.

The lift had now reached their floor. When they got out, the manager followed them.

'The signora was happy with us? The rooms were comfortable?' he asked, with charming – with touching – solicitude. 'Everything was all right?'

'Everything is very nice, thank you,' Vera said. Her mind was made up. She was going to stay. Tantalising smells were coming up from the kitchen. She was nice and hungry. And the children must be starving. To please them she uttered the word she knew would throw them into transports. 'Spaghetti!' she said. They squealed with delight, although Linda liked playing with it more than eating it. 'They love spaghetti,' she said turning to the young man. Then she took the plunge. 'I've decided to stay on – for the whole of our time here,' she said – 'the whole winter anyway,' she added scrupulously, just in case she might want to go for a few days to Rome – or maybe even Venice.

What was wrong? His face had fallen. Then, his English deserting him, he broke into a torrent of Italian. Vera's own small stock of Italian was forced to the fore. '*Non capisco!*' she said.

But Gloria had understood. 'He's telling you the hotel is closing down, Mother! It's the end of the season – they're closing *tomorrow!*'

'*Grazie, signorina,*' the manager said. His English flowed back. 'In the Spring the signora will perhaps do us the honour to return – with her delightful children.'

Return? But from where? Vera's confidence collapsed.

'It's not fair,' she cried. 'No one told me – '

The young man politely pointed to a notice in the lift. 'There are notices everywhere.' He bowed.

'In Italian I suppose,' Vera said bitterly and as even she herself knew, unfairly.

'The signora will find some place else,' the young man stated.

'But I've spent the whole fortnight looking for somewhere else!' Vera cried, losing all discretion, 'and I couldn't find anything; *anything*. Oh, what will I do? What will I do?'

'Mother, please, *please!*' Gloria pleaded. 'Think of

Linda!' she added adultly. It was too late to think of Linda however. Bursting into tears the child had thrown herself into the arms of the manager.

It looked like the end – the very, very end. In fact it was the beginning of the beginning. Falling to his knees the manager clasped Linda to his heart.

'*Tresoro mio,*' he crooned, although he could hardly be heard above Linda's wailing. Behind the child's back he held up four fingers, which, incredible as it seemed, for so young a man, Vera took to mean he had four children of his own. 'I will find you a place,' he said, and setting Linda back on her feet, after dusting down the knees of his suit, he shot a series of questions at Vera, himself supplying the answers.

'*Irlandese? Si.*

'*Profesore? Si.*

'*Catolica? Si.*'

Then he smiled. 'Tonight I telephone. I explain everything! Tomorrow morning I take you in my car!'

Linda's tears had dried. The children were all staring.

'Take us where?' Vera cried.

The young man was so pleased with himself he stepped back into the lift and closed the golden gates. He pressed the button that would carry him out of sight before replying.

'The Villa Violetta!'

It was in fact late afternoon before the manager could fulfill his promise. A chamber-maid, no longer wearing an apron, brought breakfast to their room. When she came back later to strip the beds she helped

Vera to pack. And when it was found that the manager could not take them till after lunch they were given a very good meal, not only cooked by the chef, but served by him as well, wearing a blue serge suit and a flamboyant yellow tie. The main dish was *osso buco*, and to encourage Linda to eat up, he fished a bone out of her plate and licking it clean, put it on her finger as a ring.

At four o'clock when the manager was ready at last the entire staff came to the door to wave them off, grouped as if for a photograph. Then the car drove off with them at breakneck speed.

The narrow crowded streets presented no difficulty whatever to their driver. He seemed to dive straight into a crowd as into a puddle, splashing pedestrians up to either side. And all the while the young man was scattering smiles to right and to left, and calling out greetings to other young men in other fast cars.

Soon they were out of the city, speeding along one of the large outer viales of modern Florence where villas, glimpsed through elaborate wrought iron grilles, showed glimpses of secluded gardens. Suddenly the car shot diagonally across the wide viale and, slowing down, nudged along the kerb – on the wrong side – as the young man tried to read the numbers on the gates.

'Villa Violetta!' he cried, after a few moments. And depositing them on the pavement he was about to depart and leave them there, up to their knees in luggage, when Vera gave a frightened exclamation. But the young man, mistaking this exclamation for thanks, bowed and muttering a few of the ubiquitous *pregos* which more than ever sounded to Vera like 'hey presto', jumped into his car, turned in a half-circle, and sped away.

The villa was larger than any other villa in the vicinity. Like the others it too was secluded behind a high wall over which, however, no trees showed, no creepers spilled. The ground surrounding the bleak building had been cemented over. The only ornament was a plaster statue of the Virgin, fixed to the wall. The place had the cold, repellent look of an Irish convent.

This was the worst yet. They could not stay here. But how would they get back? Vera looked around. In the distance trams clanged, but would she be able to lug the suitcases that far? And would she be allowed to take luggage on a tram? She'd have to ring the convent bell and ask the nuns to telephone for a taxi. But how would she explain her changed plans? No matter. Desperate, she pulled the bell rope.

At once the gate flew open.

'Mrs Traske? Welcome, dear!' said a warm Irish voice with a strong Galway accent. 'We were expecting you all morning. I am Sister Patrick.' A small, fat bundle of a nun scooped up their heavy cases, all of them, like a stevedore, and gathering the children tight to her with one magnetic smile, made off into the convent. 'Our Superior, Mother Brigid, will be down to welcome you herself as soon as she is free,' she said when they were inside, and she started off again ahead of them, up a big oak staircase fragrant with beeswax. On the first landing she paused. 'We are very busy today,' she said. 'We have a coach tour arriving this evening. They're not Irish, alas, but they're the next best thing – they're London-Irish.' She was starting happily up the next flight. 'This same party has been here with us for three years running. They love staying at Villa Violetta because we cater specially for them. They don't feel they're in Italy at all,' she said proudly.

Mid-way up another flight of stairs Sister Patrick put down the heaviest of the cases for a moment and looked anxiously at Vera.

'Did you have your lunch?' she asked. 'We try not to serve food between meals, but I could always – '

'Oh not at all, Sister. We had a very good lunch.'

The nun turned and stared blankly at her. 'That's something unusual in Italy, isn't it?' she then said blandly, and she glanced at the children. 'They look well though. Poor mites, the change of food is harder on them than on us.' She nodded sagaciously, ' – all the old sauces, and that dirty olive oil they use in everything. Here in Villa Violetta we *never* use olive oil. As for garlic – ' she patted Vera reassuringly, and raised her eyebrows. Picking up the cases again, she plodded on upwards.

Arriving at last on a corridor, with at least ten rooms to either side, Sister Patrick put down the cases outside a door in the middle of the corridor. 'Here we are. I'll leave you to sort your bags. Take whichever two rooms you wish,' she said, 'except that one', and she pointed to the door at the end and she suddenly lowered her voice. Vera assumed there was someone asleep, or not feeling well, so she suggested taking the two rooms near the stairs.

'The rooms on this floor are a bit on the small side,' the nun said. 'But I think you'll find they have everything you want. You have your own towels and soap, of course, haven't you?'

'Oh no,' Vera said, 'I – '

'Ah well, don't worry. We are ready for all emergencies. People are forever leaving towels behind. I'll bring some up for you. And – ' she gave Vera's arm a sympathetic pat and lowered her voice, 'I've managed to squeeze an extra table into your room. I'm sure here with us you'll settle down to your work in no time.'

Vera stared. Did the whole of Italy know her plight?

Sister Patrick was nodding her head reassuringly. 'You'll see how much better you'll feel tonight after a good homely meal.' She beamed at the children. 'We'll be having a special treat for the pilgrims – guess what? – rashers and eggs. And,' she said, turning to Vera, 'at a normal hour too – six o'clock!'

Vera's heart could sink no lower. She went into one of the rooms and sat on the bed. What next? But the children had already opened their cases and were excitedly hanging up their clothes in the small wardrobes. For them it was like playing house. She too got up and started to unpack. She had just finished when there was great activity downstairs. The London-Irish had arrived. Looking out the window they saw the big coach in the street below.

'Do you think we might get a ride in the tour bus?' Bea asked.

Vera couldn't keep back her bitterness.

'Certainly not,' she said. 'Those tours are only for – ' She stopped. She was in no position to make social distinctions. In an hour she'd be taking them down to their rashers and eggs, in a bare – and probably ugly – refectory where not a word of Italian would be heard.

At five minutes to six, however, when she led them down the stairs, it was a stream of Italian that met her.

A tall pleasant-faced priest was obviously making arrangements for the next day with the Italian coach driver whom he was seeing to the door.

'*Buona sera,* Luigi,' the priest said, closing the door. Turning around he encountered Vera and the children. 'A grand fellow – that Luigi,' he said as naturally to them as if he had known them for years. 'This is the fourth time he's taken care of us here in Italy. He meets us at the border – at Ventimiglia, and after that we don't have a care in the world.' He smiled. 'Coming to supper?' he said, and taking Linda by the hand he led the way towards the dining-hall and opened the door. His own party was already assembled, seated at a long table made up by putting together a number of smaller tables. Sister Patrick stood inside the door with an aluminium teapot as big as a kettle held in both hands.

'Good evening, Father Tom,' she said beaming happily. 'I know you're dying for a good strong cup of tea – I suppose you'll sit in your usual place?'

Father Tom laughed. 'This is the only place where I'm ever put, at top table!' he said to Vera. Then, as Sister Patrick directed Vera to a small table by the wall, he intervened. 'What's the sense of putting them over there at the other end of the earth,' he said, ' – causing unnecessary steps to yourself and the rest of the good sisters?' Taking Linda's hand again, he called out to the seated company. 'Move your chairs along there – like good people. Make room. We're having visitors tonight.' Giving Vera no time to protest he turned to Bea. 'I'm sure you can sing,' he said to her. 'You have the look of a warbler. And I make everyone sing for his supper!'

Immediately room was found for the four of them.

Sister Patrick carried their cups and saucers over from the other table.

Father Tom had made a place at the top for Vera beside himself. To her embarrassment, without lowering his voice, he began talking about the group, but glancing down the table Vera saw they were occupied with the children and were not listening.

'I insist on the singing!' the priest said. 'It keeps them out of mischief. I get them started the minute the train leaves Victoria Station, and I don't let them stop till we're back there again – except for a few hours' sleep,' he smiled, 'and a little time off for meals, of course. Seriously! We have some very good voices among us.' He pointed down the table. 'Leo there is a baritone.' He raised his voice. 'Isn't that right, Leo?'

But Sister Patrick had come around again with the teapot. 'All his geese are swans,' she said to Vera.

'Swans? When did you ever hear a swan singing? It's nightingales they are!' Father Tom said. 'Seriously,' he said again, addressing himself to Vera alone, 'Leo has a very powerful voice. He is a London bus conductor, and he has to keep very long hours, but he never fails to turn up to sing in my choir. And do you see that young girl on his left? That's Lena – hasn't she a lovely face? – Well, she has a lovely voice too.' He sighed – just a short quick sigh that might have had a physical cause. Then he went on. 'Lena has a caliper on her leg.'

Vera was listening raptly now.

'He has a grand voice himself, ma'am,' a voice called from the middle of the table, and at first Vera thought the little creature who spoke must be a circus-dwarf she was so small.

'Thank you, Maggie, thank you,' Father Tom said. 'I'd be flattered, only we all know we can't believe a word out of your mouth.' There was a roar of laughter from the whole table. The priest turned back to Vera. 'Maggie is a saint if ever there was one, she's in my parish, but she's cook in a house in Mayfair, and she has to get up at six o'clock every morning to get across London.' He paused. 'We're from Camden Town. But I suppose Sister Patrick told you our whole history?' Vera thought he looked sharply at her, and she wondered if he had been told hers. She felt her face flush, but the priest was chatting easily. 'Maggie's been in London for thirty-seven years, and in that time she has sent home all her earnings to her married sisters and brothers. She has educated eleven nieces and nephews. Not that they were ungrateful. I've met several of them, and they are a credit to Maggie. But in the twenty odd years she'd been working in London, all Maggie saw of the world was what she saw from the trains in the Underground!' He gave a short laugh – 'That is to say until I made her save a little money to come with us on our first tour. Since then she's never missed a tour.'

The nuns meanwhile were busily buzzing around the tables. Plates of bread had been replenished, and cups refilled, and for the third time Vera had to lean to one side to let Sister Patrick get between her and Father Tom with the big aluminium teapot. 'You see,' Father Tom went on, unperturbed by the fussing of the little nun, 'I started a club, and anyone who wanted to do so paid in a few bob every week. In no time at all they had saved up the price of the tour – plus a bit of spending money as well.' Suddenly he scanned the table. 'Terence,' he called out to a thin shy-looking young man sitting beside Leo, 'come up here and change places with one of the little girls. Bea? You are Bea, aren't you? Well, Bea, go down there and ask Leo to teach you how to drive a bus,' he said. When Bea hesitated, he turned to Gloria. 'You go, too,' he said. He wagged his fingers at Bea. 'Don't you come crying to me when your sister is speeding down Piccadilly at the wheel of a big red bus.' Delighted, both girls jumped up. Linda, too, started to get down from her chair.

'Linda – stay where you are!' Vera called, but her voice was lost in the rising din, and Linda ran after her sisters.

'Don't worry about her!' Father Tom said. This time his glance at her was definitely penetrating. 'You're a terrible worrier, I'm afraid. We'll have to do something about you.' His searching eyes ran over her and he seemed about to say something else but instead he frowned. 'Excuse me a minute,' he said abruptly. 'I forgot something.'

Getting up he strode over to where Sister Patrick was handing the dirty plates through the service-hatch. The priest stood talking to the nun for a few minutes, both of them obviously deeply concerned about something. Vera noticed too that a hush had come over the dining-hall, and that Leo and Maggie and several of the others had turned in their seats and were anxiously watching their priest. Yet when Father Tom came back, he appeared not to notice these enquiring looks. He sat down and apologised again for the interruption. 'I just wanted to make sure that Peggy's tray went up.' He shook his head. 'It's so odd

to think she sits up in bed and eats her meals quite
normally as if there was nothing the matter!' Seeing
that Vera didn't know what he was talking about he
looked surprised. 'Didn't Sister Patrick tell you? We
had an accident in Rome – we are nearing the end of
our second week in Italy, you know.' Lines of
worry furrowed his face. 'I suppose I couldn't expect
to have gone on indefinitely without some hitch, but
this business of Peggy is so unusual. It's not like a
real accident at all – it's – '

'But what happened?' Vera asked, feeling that if she
had been less absorbed in her own problems, Sister
Patrick might have told her. 'Don't tell me – if it dis-
tresses you,' she added, because she now saw as well as
looking worried, the priest looked very tired.

'On the contrary, it's a relief to talk about it – ' he
said, 'to someone else besides this mob. If I let them,
they'd talk about nothing else – which does no good
to anyone.' He sighed. 'We had only arrived in Rome –
it was our first day there, and Luigi was taking us
round the Vatican. We always begin with St. Peter's,
and we were finishing up the morning with a visit to
the dome. Peggy's mother was the only one who didn't
go up. She didn't say why – and we didn't bother to
ask. She's a quiet little woman, a widow, and Peggy is
her only child. I think it was for Peggy's sake she came
on the tour – not for her own sake at all. Well anyway,
we left her sitting in a café just beyond St. Peter's
Square and we all went up in the lift to the dome. I
myself hate going up in that lift, but the others love it,
and of course I always feel it's worth it when we get to
the top and look out over that immense panorama.'
He sighed again. 'Well, when we got out of the lift and

stood on the platform, there were the usual gasps and exclamations. It makes me gasp myself, the first sight of those towers and domes, but afterwards I distinctly remembered having noticed that Peggy was over-excited.

' "Oh look, look," she cried, although, being small like her mother, she could hardly see beyond the para-pet. "Can you find my mother?" she cried. "Let me look. I want to wave to her." She pushed her way to the front, but I still think she could only barely have seen over the top when quite suddenly her face went dead-white. I knew she was going to faint. In Camden Town we're used to people fainting at Mass. The church gets very hot and stuffy, especially in summer. I was not greatly worried. I was just glad I was near and able to catch her before she fell. Leo and Maggie held her head down and fanned her face, but after a few seconds I realised she was not coming round as quickly as she ought.

' "Get her mother up here," I told them. I wasn't even thinking of a doctor at that stage. But Terence, who went to fetch the mother, came back without her.

' "The mother won't come up", he said. "She's in an awful state, Father. She says she's afraid of heights. She says – " '

Here Father Tom looked at Vera. 'You've guessed? Fear of heights – congenital at that – vertigo you know. One is inclined to treat it lightly, but there are people who'd let themselves be cut into pieces before they'd go up on a height or look over a cliff – and Peggy was one. The mother was one too, but she was aware of her condition. She just didn't know about Peggy. Neither did Peggy herself. I realised im-

mediately then that we were in for something serious.
The girl's whole system had suffered an enormous
shock in that moment when she looked down. I didn't
lose any more time, I can tell you. I had a doctor up
there in a matter of minutes, although I had to raise hell
to get one so quickly. The Vatican guards must have
thought someone had jumped off the parapet, and I'm
afraid I didn't disabuse them until I saw the doctor
himself appear. Anyway, the poor girl might as well
have fallen. She was in a deep coma. They got her to
hospital and called in a specialist at once. She came out
of the coma next day all right, but it was then the real
trouble began. At first they didn't know she had come
out of it. She didn't speak, you see, or make any sign.
She couldn't be got to utter a word. She showed no
recognition of anyone, her mother, or Maggie, or me.
There was absolutely no communicating with her.'
The priest looked at Vera. 'In every respect, other
than what I've told you, she is perfectly normal. She
eats, drinks, sleeps, and is clearly conscious of what is
going on. She doesn't get out of bed, of course, but
there is no reason why she should not. Frankly, we
feel she's probably safer there till we can get her home
and have the London doctors look at her.'

Vera remembered what he had said earlier about
sending a tray upstairs. 'Where is she now?'

Father Tom sighed. 'She's here with us – she's upstairs. Naturally my first instinct was to send her home
– to send both of them home, the mother and the girl.
The Red Cross would probably have given assistance,
but anyway there'd have been no shortage of money:
we'd have raised a fund among ourselves. We couldn't
have let them go alone though, someone would have

had to travel with them. And of course I would have been the obvious choice. Yet I simply could not see the others getting on without me. Remember the tour was only starting then!'

Vera glanced down the table. 'It would have been out of the question,' she agreed.

Father Tom too looked down the table.

'God love them!' he said. 'Do you know what they suggested – that we'd *all* go back and give up the tour altogether. Imagine that! A whole year of their savings had been sunk in it. But I had an idea and I spoke to her doctor in Rome, and he thought my plan was feasible enough. What I suggested was that we'd carry on with the tour as planned, except that Peggy would stay in bed while we were out sightseeing and the mother would stay with her. Anyway we tried it out for that week in Rome and it worked all right. Then, when we were coming here we sent them on ahead by ambulance. I telephoned Sister Patrick and explained. We are hoping to carry on in the same way for the remaining few days. They'll stay here in Villa Violetta while we go off on our day trips. We hope to see Sienna tomorrow, and Fiesole the next day, finishing up with Assisi. I haven't quite worked out the plans for our journey home, but I think we'll follow the same procedure: send her by ambulance to Ventimiglia, and from there, with sleepers, or possibly a private compartment, we'll manage the journey home. Or we might drastically alter our plans and take the train home from here. It would be a bit disappointing for Luigi – a departure from our custom – but he is just as upset about Peggy as we are ourselves, and he'd understand.'

Luigi might understand but Vera was lost, and realising it, Father Tom explained further.

'Our first trip was a pilgrimage to Lourdes, but this is our fourth time to Italy. The first time we came by train all the way and used coaches only in Rome and Florence. Luigi owned the coach here in Florence and when we were leaving he suggested that if we were coming another year he'd meet us at the border and we could do all the internal travelling in Italy with him in his coach. And at the end he'd take us back to Ventimiglia. But the more I think about our problem with Peggy, the wiser it seems to get on the train here in Florence – all of us.' He sighed. 'These are minor details though, and of course I am worried all the time in case I am making a mistake handling things this way at all. I am just following my instinct, and that is always a risk, isn't it? This way is certainly easier on the girl's mother, and when we get back to London she'll have all of us at hand to help her. It's hard to believe the London specialists won't come up with some treatment that will bring the girl round. What do you think?'

'I think you probably did the best you could,' Vera said, 'and I suppose there's always the chance that here, with so many people she knows around her, she might suddenly snap out of it.'

Father Tom shook his head.

'I thought that too at the beginning. I'm afraid it was over-optimistic. We can be thankful that we had Villa Violetta to come to. The hostel in Rome was run by nuns too. We couldn't have kept her with us in an ordinary hotel. Here there's always someone to keep an eye on her and give the poor mother a respite. The

I

nuns are good with the mother too. They offered to look after Peggy all day tomorrow so she could come with us to Sienna. But she's very sensitive, and she knows she'd be a dampener on the others.'

Here something made him break off and look at Vera. 'I've just thought of something. Those two empty places in the coach! Why don't you let two of the older children come with us tomorrow? They'd have a wonderful trip, and we'd take good care of them. They'd be off your hands all day and you'd have time to yourself. I understand you're here on a Fellowship? You can't be getting much work done?'

So, Sister Patrick had said something about her! Vera hesitated before replying. Her hesitation seemed only to confirm some opinion the priest had formed of her.

'That settles it,' he said, ' – except – ' he seemed to be making some rapid calculation, 'I don't see why we can't take all three children while we're at it. If necessary, the little one could sit on someone's knee.'

'Oh Father!' Vera could hardly speak. She had not had one hour to herself – not one minute – since she'd left home. In a whole day, what might she not accomplish?

She got up from the table and smiled down at him.

'I'd better get them to bed,' she said. 'I'm sure you like to make an early start?'

'That's a good girl,' he said. 'Breakfast at seven-thirty! But wait a minute. Why don't you just put the little one to bed, and let the older ones stay up for a while and join in our sing-song? Go on! It won't hurt them. The minute I saw them in the hall I thought they could do with some fun.'

Vera bit her lip. It was true. But would she be able

to get Linda to go to bed alone? Father Tom, however, had called out something to Leo. The next minute
Linda was on Leo's back going out of the dining-hall,
happily blowing back kisses to everyone.

Leo carried the child all the way up the stairs. Vera
had only to follow. When they reached her floor and
were going along their own corridor Vera remembered
the room that was closed and she looked curiously
down the corridor. As if she'd spoken Leo nodded.

'Yes, that's her room,' he said.

'Whose room?' Linda demanded.

'Nobody's!' Vera snapped, but she knew immediately she'd been unwise to focus attention on it, so
when Leo put the child down she started to tell her
about the next day's excursion to Sienna.

'In the coach?' Linda cried incredulously. Her smile
was ecstatic.

Next morning when Vera had waved the party off,
standing on the steps beside Sister Patrick, she went up
to her room hopefully prepared to open her brief-case
and take out her papers. But there were so many small
personal chores to be done that she'd had no time for
since she left home, she felt she had better attend
to them first. She washed her hair and did her nails,
and sewed missing buttons on the girls' coats, as well
as one on the jacket of her own suit and she also fixed
a torn hem on her skirt. It shocked her to think how
she'd been letting her appearance go. Then after lunch
she took out the map of Florence again to try to es-
tablish her new position, but Sister Patrick came along
while she was struggling with it. Like Carlotta, the nun
also took the Duomo as focal point.

'That's the trouble, Sister! I never can find it. I lose my way in those narrow streets.'

Sister Patrick looked at her in astonishment. 'But it can be seen from everywhere,' she said, 'like Nelson's Pillar in Dublin. You've only to look up!'

Vera laughed heartily, but she knew her trouble with the Duomo was over.

'Thank you, Sister,' she said fervently, and venturing out later in the afternoon she found indeed that the Duomo was harder to lose than to find. Greatly heartened, when the coach came back she was on the steps to meet the children.

'Oh Mother, you should have come,' they cried.

Vera's mind was filled with visions of the rolling Tuscan hills as she'd known them when she was here with their father. She was glad his children had seen them too, in spite of her failures.

'Oh, Mother,' Bea cried, speaking for all three, 'we went up a *huge* hill, to a *tiny* little town – '

'Certaldo,' Father Tom put in, 'between here and Sienna.'

' – and what do you think, Mother, there was this writer – '

'Boccaccio,' Father Tom said dryly.

' – and there was this priest who dug up his bones and threw them down the hill – '

'In 1783!' Father Tom said. 'Don't hold it against me.'

Bea looked put out by the interruptions, but she went on.

' – only a kind lady – '

'A wealthy American lady,' Father Tom said.

' – went down and picked up the bones and put them in a box and – '

'A casket,' Father Tom was finding it hard to keep a straight face.

'I can see you all had a great day,' Vera said. She gave Bea a hug.

'Do you know what we had for our lunch, Mother? We had – '

Father Tom put his hand firmly over Bea's mouth.

'No more of that,' he said, 'or Sister Patrick will think we don't need any supper.'

Leo who had joined them, was clearly in thrall to Linda.

'She got me to eat spaghetti,' he said, and he pretended to wind long strings of pasta on to an imaginary fork as if the fork was a windlass.

'Leo, you could give lessons to Luigi!' Father Tom said laughing, but the next minute he left them and bounded up the stairs. To see Peggy, Vera guessed.

When the priest returned everyone was seated in the dining-room. He sat down beside Vera and took up the conversation where he'd left off.

'The food was so good in Sienna,' he said. 'When I am planning these tours I never skimp on the meals. All along the way I've managed to arrange for four-star restaurants.' He laughed. 'I'd have liked five-star only they don't cater for coach-tours.' He glanced around to see if Sister Patrick was out of earshot. 'It's by sleeping in places like this – friendly and clean but not very exciting – that we can afford to eat our mid-day meal at top-class restaurants. And if occasionally some of the party don't like the foreign food, I know they can look forward to the good homely meals they'll get here when they return in the evening.' The nuns were taking out hot platters from the hatch. He sniffed. 'Irish stew tonight! See what I mean? I'm really sorry you weren't in Sienna with us. We had the famous Sienna dish *Buristo Suino* – do you know it? – it's lean pork cooked with all kinds of nuts and raisins and chunks of fat, and it has a strange piney flavour – and of course the wine was the local Brolio. By the way, I gave the children some wine – diluted with water. I hope that was all right? I can't tell you how much we enjoyed having them. Bea has a beautiful voice. And the little one is a charmer. I hope you'll let them come with us again tomorrow? We're going to Fiesole – for the whole day.'

'They'd love it, I'm sure,' Vera said.

Then, casually, the priest asked another question.

'What did you do today, Vera?'

Vera looked away. She suspected he'd guessed that she'd done no real work.

'I got lots of odds and ends of things done,' she said defensively, and then she stopped.

The priest looked keenly at her. 'Now's your chance, you know. We'll be here for two more days – and we'll be delighted to take the children with us: they're part of the outfit now. You needn't feel under any compliment either – I am grateful to you for lending them to us. They more than pulled their weight. I didn't realise how much of my time I gave to these folks: they are like children themselves at times, all demanding their share of personal attention. In the coach I usually have to sit with a different one each day. But this afternoon, coming back from Sienna no one took any notice of me at all. I was able to do something I've always wanted – sit up front with Luigi. I had the most restful day of the whole trip. And look now,' he added, nodding down the table, 'you can see for yourself they've forgotten all about me.' Compared with the previous night, Vera could see that his parishioners were indeed making less demands on him. The children were the centre of attention.

'Quiet, everybody,' Leo called out just then. 'Linda is going to give us a song.'

Vera raised her eyebrows. 'Linda is no prima donna.'

'Oh, that doesn't matter,' Father Tom said. 'At that age it is their lack of self-consciousness that is enchanting.' Then, as Linda's childish voice tinkled out, Father Tom sighed. 'I love children,' he said and Vera was surprised at the depth of feeling in his voice. 'People don't realise it, but as we priests get older, it is the loss of paternity that is the hardest part of celibacy.'

They were both silent for a moment.

'What made you become a priest, Father?' Vera asked quietly. The priest did not seem surprised at her question.

'Mine was a late vocation,' he said. 'I'd gone into the bank originally. I was nearly thirty when I went to the seminary, and I was thirty-five when I was ordained.' He paused, and not wishing to appear to force a confidence Vera said nothing. 'You see, I was going to marry a girl who was working in the Bank with me.' He looked down at the table for a moment, then he looked up. 'She died. She was killed in an accident the week before we were to be married.'

It was so unexpected a story Vera gave a slight gasp. 'Surely in time,' she murmured, 'you would have – '

' – met someone who would have filled her place? Is that what you mean?' He stared down into his empty tea-cup. 'I suppose I would. In fact, I know I would – and before long in all likelihood.' Then he looked up at her, his strong blue eyes uncompromising and sure. 'But I didn't want to fill her place – ever – ' Then he smiled ' – except with this mob,' he said. 'They've certainly filled my life, but not I think in a way Agnes – that was her name – would have minded.'

Impulsively Vera laid her hand on his sleeve. 'She must be smiling down at you from heaven,' she said, although such sentimentality was altogether uncharacteristic of her.

'More likely laughing at me,' Father Tom said, and fearing she might have embarrassed him, Vera changed the conversation.

'You said you worked in a bank?'

He was obviously grateful to her for turning the conversation. 'Yes, I was assistant manager. That's why I'm so slick at arranging these tours. The travel agents aren't prepared for a clergyman who drives a hard bargain. And this mob can't get over the good value I get for them. I'm up to all kinds of dodges. I told you they pay in a small sum every week. Well, a small sum from a lot of people is no longer small. Right? The minute I get their weekly contributions I put the money into the bank to start earning interest immediately. So at the end of the year, these good people have a somewhat larger sum than they know, and I am able to arrange for little extras like first-class seats in the train and – as I've already told you – the very best restaurants, and so on – ' Here he paused, and it seemed to Vera that his face took on an earnestness out of proportion to the context until, abruptly, he turned to her. 'What is your problem, Vera?' he asked. 'I mean – your special problem here in Florence – apart from the obvious one of being a widow with three children – ?'

She was completely taken aback.

'Is it so obvious? Or did Sister Patrick speak to you about me?'

Father Tom raised his eyebrows. 'Sister Patrick? She's far too busy to *talk* about people's problems. She has her hands filled with solving them. No, she didn't tell me anything. No one did. But I have eyes in my head. What is wrong, Vera? You told me you had a Fellowship. I should have thought that would have dispelled some of your worries.'

'So would I!' Vera said. 'That was my first mistake. I thought that here in Italy, with someone else paying for our board and lodging, I'd have been able to get so much done.' She shook her head and looked down miserably.

'And?' Father Tom said.

She shook her head again. 'It's much worse here than at home. At home I could at least work while they were at school, but so far here I haven't had a chance even to look for a school – ' She sat up. 'That's what I should have done yesterday.'

'Vera!' Father Tom's voice was stern. 'What exactly did you do yesterday?'

'Well, I – '

'You did nothing!' the priest said bluntly. 'You're obviously in no condition to work. What you need is a complete rest. And so – you are going to be kidnapped – tomorrow – by me. *You* are going to come with us to Fiesole as well as the children.' As she started to protest he put up his hands. 'I'll take no excuses. I know quite well that a coach tour with me and this lot is not your idea of the proper way to see Italy. But I have a plan, and as I've already told you, I'm not bad with other people's problems. Will you trust me, Vera? Will you come?'

Cautiously Vera lifted her head and looked into the blue eyes that were staring so hard at her.

'We're going first to Fiesole,' Father Tom said matter-of-factly. 'We're doing a little sight-seeing, but we're going there principally to have lunch at one of the best restaurants in Italy. After lunch we are coming back through Florence again and up into the hills on the other side – to Scandicci – because Luigi – ' He broke off. 'You haven't met Luigi yet? He's a mar- vellous fellow – I've known him for four years, and I feel as if he was one of my parishioners. There is very little I don't know about him and his family. By the way, what age would you say he was? My age? Your age?' He laughed. 'I'll tell you. He's old enough to be our father. He is a grandfather! He had six children of his own and he reared all six of them single-handed. His wife died when the youngest was only a year old. They did very well for themselves too. The older ones went to work early and helped him out with the younger ones. Of course the younger ones got the best of it. They all got special training, and Luigi and the older ones helped start them out in careers. And when it came to the youngest one – ' but here Father Tom laughed as if at himself – 'well, it's because of Luigi's youngest son that we're going to Scandicci tomorrow night! I told you I was always on the alert for good value. Well, Luigi's son has opened a restaurant up there. Luigi helped to set him up and I was able to arrange credit for them. He's doing very well. The restaurant is rapidly getting a name for good food. People are coming out from Florence for lunch on Sundays – and he's had a number of bookings for weddings and christenings. So far it's only Italians who know the place. Massimo – that's the young man's name – has not yet got well enough known to attract the tourists, and so he's very pleased to have a coach-load of us for a meal. That's where we're having dinner.' He put his hand on her arm. 'I'd like very much if you'd come, Vera, if only for the sake of that dinner! I can promise you it will be one of the best you've ever eaten. Luigi will see to that. And of course it will give added pleasure to him and to Massimo – and to all of us – if you come.' He paused. 'What about it?'

Before she could reply Linda's song came to an end. Everyone at the table seemed to have heard the priest's invitation.

'*Please* come, Mrs Traske,' Leo said.

'*Please*,' Maggie begged.

'*Please, please, please,* Mother,' said Gloria, Bea and Linda.

'You couldn't hold out against entreaties like that. It's settled: you'll come,' Father Tom stood up. 'A sleep-in tomorrow for anyone who likes,' he announced. 'You too, Leo. One of the nuns can serve my Mass. Luigi won't be here until ten.' He turned back to Vera. 'I have to slip up now and see Peggy's mother. Will you excuse me?'

'How is she?'

'Peggy – or the mother?' he asked, vaguely. His voice was suddenly very tired. He probably had the sick girl continually on his mind although he was too disciplined to show it.

'We'll see you in the morning, Father,' Vera said, glad she'd given him pleasure by her decision to go with them.

Morning brought the most perfect day Vera and the children had in Italy. The sun came streaming through the slatted windows of the refectory at Villa Violetta, and breakfast was over almost as soon as it began. Everyone was anxious to be off. There was a steady coming and going in the hall as people went back to their rooms for things they had forgotten. But well before ten they were all assembled in the hall. And when Sister Patrick opened the big front door Luigi had already arrived with the coach.

'This is a big day for Luigi,' Father Tom reminded them.

Luigi was plainly in great fettle. He had jumped down from his seat and was helping everyone into the coach.

'Are you *sure* there is a seat for me?' Vera asked uneasily.

'Do you want to cry off?' Father Tom asked, looking keenly at her.

Vera shook her head, surprised to find that she was looking forward to the day.

'Luigi!' Father Tom called out. 'The signora will sit up front with you.'

As the coach moved off Vera began to appreciate the privilege of sitting up front. As they cruised through the crowded streets it was like riding in a chariot. Below them even the most dashing Lagondas and Lancias looked lowly and earth-bound. And when they left Florence behind and began to climb towards Fiesole, she was as excited as the children.

The coach now had to make its way up roads so steep and narrow between the walled villas that at every minute Vera expected to hear the sides scratch against the wall. But no – they cruised smoothly along, and even when another coach approached them, coming downwards, the two great ships of the tarmac passed each other as easily as liners in the immensity of the ocean. On these occasions Luigi and the other driver saluted each other with a toot on the horn.

Vera found herself regretting she had not gone with them the previous day to Sienna. Luigi was a superb guide. He didn't confine himself to pointing out items of interest to tourists, but all along the way different things struck sparks from his memory, and he related anecdotes of his childhood, his family, his relations and his friends.

They were just entering Fiesole when he slowed down almost to a stop and pointed to a small house on the side of the hill.

'That is where I brought my wife Conceptione when we were first married,' he said. 'That is where our children were born, and that is where Conceptione died.'

'Is it where you live now?' Vera asked, trying to hide her surprise, because the house, although small, had a great air of elegance.

Luigi shook his head. 'No,' he said. 'Fiesole is no longer for such as us. Fiesole for the wealthy man. Last year Father Tom make me sell. Now I live on the other side of the Arno. Not fashionable. But bigger villa.

Cheaper price. More land. Better investment!' He wagged his head happily at his own and the priest's wiles. 'Scandicci not fashionable, but Scandicci beautiful. Fiesole for the past; Scandicci for the future.'

'I'm longing to see it,' Vera murmured.

'*Si, si.*' Luigi's face beamed. 'My son Massimo get first prize in hotel-course in Switzerland. Tonight you see Villa. *Magnifico.* Father Tom say my Massimo will "put Scandicci on the map".' Proud of his slang, he repeated it, ' "put Scandicci on the map". Massimo cheaper prices than restaurants in Fiesole or Florence – because in Scandicci rates not so high. People like to go out in the country for a good meal – yes?'

'Oh yes, yes.' Vera herself was looking forward to the meal. Several times during the afternoon as they went in and out of churches, she'd found herself thinking of Massimo's villa and of the vineyards and the olive groves Luigi had described. And even the excellent lunch in Fiesole had not curbed her appetite for the coming meal in Scandicci. She wondered if Father Tom for once had arranged for a midday meal less copious than usual?

'What does your son call his restaurant?' she asked when, having seen the last of Fiesole, they dipped down again into the valley that was Florence, and crossed the Arno, to wind into the hills on the other side.

Luigi seemed astonished at the question.

'Ristorante Massimo,' he said.

But now from close behind her, Vera heard Father Tom's voice.

'It's the tradition here that a great chef gives his name to his restaurant,' he explained, and Vera saw that the priest had changed his seat, and was now sitting in a seat right behind her. He would, of course, want to catch the very first glimpse of the property he had been instrumental in buying.

'Would you not change places with me, Father?' she asked, feeling that he and Luigi might want to talk business. He shook his head, and in fact Luigi answered for him.

'Father Tom saw it last year. I took him up here.'

'That was when we hatched the plan,' Father Tom said. 'I only needed one look at the villa, and one look at the view, and that, combined with my confidence in Massimo's ability – he has a portfolio full of diplomas – left me with no doubts at all about Luigi's wisdom in backing the venture.'

They were steadily climbing all the time, and as well as that, wherever the road forked, Luigi was taking the smaller and steeper of the ways offered. Now they were flanked on either side by vineyards and olive groves, with only here and there an occasional villa. Below lay Florence, the late sunlight still gilding its domes and cupolas but in the gardens and public parks the blue of evening was gathering into pools.

'Oh, what a wonderful view,' Vera cried. The singing at the back of the coach had stopped. There was almost complete silence in the coach.

'It's not the view that has silenced them,' Father Tom whispered. 'It's suspense. They can't wait to meet Massimo and see his Villa.' He was excited himself too. Suddenly throwing a leg over the back of the front seat he squeezed in between Vera and Luigi. 'It's a bit of a squash, but we're nearly there,' he said, leaning forward and peering through the windscreen. Even before Luigi, Father Tom saw the restaurant and gave a shout.

Vera too leaned forward, pressing her forehead against the glass. The road had forked once more and this time, like the delta of a river, between the two roads was a village. It was a small village with only two or three dwellings, all humble, so the large pink villa in the middle *had* to be Massimo's establishment. It was certainly old, and certainly beautiful, but it was the setting that was breathtaking. To one side the hill still climbed, cross-stitched all over with vine, and in the dusk the olive trees were barely discernible, grey ghosts of their daylight selves. To the left was a valley so deep it might have been the Valley of Jehosophat, were it not for the lights of Florence which had begun to glimmer in its depths.

'Look! The whole village is waiting for us,' Father Tom said, and she saw that everywhere, from the houses, men, women and children were coming out, and standing on the side of the road to watch their arrival. 'Well, not absolutely everyone,' he said then laughing, and he pointed to a wooden cow-byre where by the light of an oil lamp hanging from a beam, two women in black were milking cows. 'They're nuns! There is a little convent up the road: the nuns run the local school.'

As the coach drew nearer to the villa, Luigi could contain himself no longer. He blew the horn. Instantly, at the sound, lights flashed on all over the place, and a handsome young man came running down the steps.

'Massimo!' cried Luigi, as if he had not seen him for twenty years. 'My son!' he announced, and he brought

the coach to a stop. Tears of pride were streaming
down his cheeks.

'Well?' Father Tom said to Vera as he helped her
down.

'The view alone would have made it worth while
coming all the way from Dublin,' she said.

Luigi was slapping Massimo on the back.

'My son, I hope you have things ready? The best
of everything!'

'*Si – si!*' said Massimo, and he turned to Vera.
'Please pass this way!' he said, and he himself went back
to welcome the others.

When they went inside, Vera was almost dazzled by
the big electrically lit chandelier that hung in the
centre of the dining-room, but she was astonished to
find that in spite of the glare within, the view through
the uncurtained windows still dominated the room.
She was drawn irresistibly to the window.

'It's what I *thought* Italy would be like,' she said.

'That is what I hoped to hear you say,' Father Tom
said. He turned to Luigi. 'I wonder would Massimo
mind letting the Signora see his own apartment?' He
turned back to Vera. 'Massimo is getting married next
Spring. His fiancée is studying hotel management.
She's taking the same course he took in Switzerland.
But Massimo has everything ready for their marriage.
Isn't that so?' he asked of Massimo who had just
joined them. 'Your father says you have made a great
job of the upstairs rooms – a new bathroom, new wall-
paper, new furniture – everything?'

Massimo nodded proudly. 'All the furniture is
antico.'

'How lovely for her,' Vera said politely.

K

'Just a minute,' Father Tom said, and he called Leo. 'Leo, the cloakrooms are on the left. Get everyone organised. I imagine the meal is ready, but I want to show Mrs Traske something.' Unexpectedly then he called Gloria and Bea. 'Would you like to come with us, girls?' he asked.

The two girls had been hanging one on each of Leo's arms, and Vera had a moment of uneasiness. Had she let them impose too much on him? The truth was she'd forgotten all about them.

'Where is Linda? Get her at once and bring her with you,' Vera said crossly – and again quite unfairly – to Gloria.

'Oh, leave Linda where she is,' Father Tom said impatiently. 'She wouldn't be interested.' So it had not been to reprimand her he had called the older girls?

'Come on,' he said, shepherding the girls and herself to the door. 'We must get this over quickly. Chefs have killed themselves before now because their food wasn't treated with proper respect! Isn't this the way?' he asked of Massimo, and preceded them all towards the stairs. 'You're not living up here yet yourself, Massimo, are you?'

As if the question was almost indelicate Massimo blushed: Luigi had to answer for him.

'Massimo still lives with Pappa,' he said, and he winked. Through a window on the landing he pointed out a small annexe at the back of the villa. Then they went up the rest of the way, and Massimo opened a door and reached for the light switch.

'Oh please, don't turn on the light – not for a minute,' Vera cried, and she ran over to the window. 'It's like looking out of a window in heaven.' She saw with delight that below in Florence all the well-known buildings, and even the bridges, were floodlit, glittering like constellations: the Duomo, the Uffizi, the Pitti Palace, the Trinita. She felt suddenly that at last, and this time forever, Florence was printed on her mind in a starry map. And when Father Tom came and stood beside her she could feel that he too was deeply stirred. But to Massimo the view was only of secondary importance. He switched on the light.

'You see, Massimo did not make the view!' Luigi said apologetically.

Vera smiled understandingly and gave her full attention to the room. 'Has your fiancée seen it yet, Massimo?'

'Not yet,' Massimo said.

'She'll love it,' Vera said, and as Bea had tiptoed over and opened a door that led into a bathroom that was all pink – pink tiles, pink tub, pink everything, she felt she could disclose to the girls what she had herself been told. 'It's a bridal suite!' she whispered.

The girls' faces broke into blissful smiles.

'Where is the bride? When is the wedding? Can we come? Can we throw confetti?' they clamoured. The thrill in their voices made the adults all smile.

Then, with the same unexpectedness that had surprised her twice already that day, Father Tom switched off the light. 'I just wanted you to see it,' he said to Vera. 'Thank you, Massimo. Now we will sample your cooking.'

Leading them down the stairs and into the dining-room where the others were already seated, Father Tom took his place at the head of the table and said grace. Then he raised his voice. 'When your glasses are filled,' he said, 'I will ask you to drink a toast to our host Massimo, and offer him our best wishes for the success of his restaurant!'

At once, as from the wings of a stage, a bevy of waiters rushed out with bottles of Asti Spumante and began to fill their glasses. While this was being done the priest excused himself and left the table. He took Luigi and Massimo out to the hall where Vera could see them talking earnestly together. When he came back the glasses had been filled, and the priest gave them the toast of Massimo. Then he sat down, and ignoring the din around him, he turned to Vera.

'I wanted the girls as well as you, to see Massimo's apartment, Vera. I had a special reason. What did you think of it? Did you notice how large it was? And there is a smaller room opening off it that I didn't ask him to show you, but it has been done up also. I thought that it would be perfect for – ' But he stopped. 'I told you I used to work in a bank, didn't I? Well, I'm afraid I'll never lose the marks of it: I can't resist trying to accommodate people. I just had a word with Luigi and Massimo – and I put it to them that you and the children were finding it hard to get somewhere to stay and that – '

'Oh but – '

'Easy now!' Father Tom said. 'Wait till I finish. Massimo's marriage won't take place till the late Spring – nearly summer – but although he has everything ready, he naturally does not wish to let the rooms – to strangers, that is to say – but as I put it to them – it would be a very different matter to allow the signora Irlandese and her daughters to occupy them over the winter – the rooms would be kept aired, but above all,

God would surely shower down His blessings on their future home for giving shelter to the signora and the children who otherwise – ' Father Tom's eye twinkled '– I'm afraid I painted an exaggerated picture of your plight. Anyway, the long and the short of it is that they agreed – both of them. They were very amenable to the suggestion. The rooms are yours, Vera, if you want them.'

'Oh but – ' Vera began.

'Wait till I finish,' the priest repeated. 'You would, of course, be their guest. There would be no question of payment.'

'Oh but – ' Vera began again. Then helplessly she began to laugh. Her first fear had been that she might become involved in too great an expense. Now her concern was that she would be taking advantage of these people. 'How could I accept that?' she cried.

Father Tom put up his hand. 'Don't worry. They are not fools, Luigi or Massimo – and I myself would not let them do anything foolish either. You would, of course, pay for your meals here in the restaurant – the same as anyone else, and at the normal price – which is not cheap – though I *did* arrange that the children would only pay for half portions. This will mean a certain fixed sum coming in for Massimo during the slack part of the week, and besides, it will be good for his business that the '*straniere*' are dining here *every* night. You'll see! They won't lose by it! And where you are concerned I've taken something else into consideration: the children can go to school at the little convent run by those nuns we saw. They'll be kept out of mischief all day, and become fluent in Italian.' He grinned. 'They might even learn to milk a cow!'

The matter had obviously been already settled though, because from the far end of the room Massimo gave Vera a knowing smile. Suddenly she felt an immense sense of security, of being cared for and protected. The fear which had never quite left her from the hour Richard died – and which, since she came to Italy, had increased to dangerous proportions – was no more. Thinking back to the day she had set out so hopefully from Dublin, she wondered what had happened to make her panic. Had she in some strange way duplicated the circumstances that had followed immediately upon Richard's sudden death? Being cut off once again, as then, from all that was familiar, alone with the children, and having to cope with new money worries, had she perhaps set up echoes of that terrible time? In these terrible days well-wishers, proffering advice, had only accentuated her aloneness, and sometimes she'd thought she sensed that some of those who tried to guide her life into new channels – women in particular – had unconsciously been envious of her when Richard was alive – that besides having a husband and a family, she had had a successful career as well. They may even have been glad to think she'd been taken down a peg. And here too in Florence her advisers meant well – even Carlotta – but the effect on her was the same. She'd felt pushed about and it was that which made her panic. But now this wise priest, with a power to help that came from complete selflessness – had given her back her confidence. Certain that his plan for her was right, certain that she now had the confidence to carry it out, she turned to him.

'When can we come?'

Father Tom didn't have to give this any thought.

'Tomorrow is the last full day of our tour,' he said. 'We are going to Assisi. Why don't you come with us? The children will love it, and I will enjoy your company. You can practise your Italian with Luigi too – and then on Saturday morning, when our tour comes to an end, Luigi can put your luggage in the coach, and you and the children can come with us to the station, and, after you've given us a send-off, you can all go home together with Luigi to Scandicci.'

Home! Vera thought of the warm-hearted peasants who had come out to wave when the coach arrived. She thought of the happy faces of Luigi and Massimo. And she thought too of the beautiful room upstairs, looking out over the Arno valley, and she could almost have cried with relief. She glanced at her children. Gloria and Bea were chatting with two young girls, cousins of Massimo not much older than themselves, who were still at school, but helped in the restaurant in their spare time. They would be friends for her girls. Vera's relief was immense. And at that moment, from the other end of the table, Linda's voice reached her.

'Cows give milk,' the child said. 'Who gives wine?'

'*Il Signor Dio,*' one of the waiters replied, but Massimo who was listening shook his head.

'The good God gives the grape,' he said. 'Man must make the wine.' He leant over Linda's chair. 'You have never seen the pressing of the grape? Next month we will have the Vendemmia. You will take off your shoes and press the grape with us – like this – I'll show you –'

Vera's heart expanded with joy; her children were in Italy at last. And, released from the world of her fears, she too was there with them.

'How can I ever thank you, Father, for what you've done for us?'

Father Tom smiled at her. 'You never know – you may someday. Nothing is ever lost.' Although like her he must have known that after Saturday it would be unlikely they would meet again.

It was later than usual when the coach arrived back at Villa Violetta and Luigi brought it alongside the darkened convent. The only light was in the porter's lodge where Sister Patrick was waiting up for them. Vera was preparing to take the children straight upstairs with the others when Father Tom stopped her.

'You won't need to supervise them tonight. They'll be asleep in no time. Linda is nearly asleep already.' Linda, thumb in mouth, and without being told to do so, was already plodding up the stairs. 'I think Sister Patrick might be persuaded to give you and me a cup of tea.'

Vera hesitated, but Sister Patrick had already rushed off into the kitchen regions. The priest opened the door of the big dining-hall that was in total darkness, and he switched on a small wall-lamp that lit only the near end of the long table and the white cups and saucers already laid out for breakfast. The light made no real impression on the darkness of the large room, and their footsteps seemed so loud in the silence that they sat down quickly. Vera wondered if the priest had something in particular about which he wanted to talk, but when they sat down he said absolutely nothing. Far off, and high up in the convent, various sounds could be heard, as his parishioners went along the corridors, and as bathroom doors opened and shut. But minute by minute these sounds were diminishing, and soon there would be absolute silence.

Vera wished that she had not agreed to have the tea. She didn't really want it – it would keep her awake. And when, after another few minutes, there was no sign of Sister Patrick, she wondered if the nun perhaps had forgotten all about it?

Then, abrupt as a falling star and as bright, from somewhere overhead there came a peal of laughter. Linda? Vera sprang to her feet.

'I should have gone up with her and made sure she went to bed.'

Father Tom was conscience-stricken. 'I would have sworn they'd be asleep in a second, after such a strenuous day.'

Vera was tired out herself. 'When children are over-tired they don't go to sleep at all,' she said wearily, and although now she heard footsteps and the rattle of cups, and knew that Sister Patrick was coming with the tea, she ran out of the room, flinging back a word of apology in case she might not be able to come downstairs again.

When she was halfway up the stairs the laugh came again. It was unmistakably Linda's laugh and just before Vera reached the landing there was yet another peal. Then predictably she could distinctly hear bare feet scurrying along the corridor, and a door slammed. Linda knew she was coming and had hopped into bed. As was to be expected, when Vera reached the top of the stairs there was absolute silence – well, not absolute, because from one room there was a sound of snoring – loud, like the snoring of a man. It was not Linda she blamed so much as the two older girls, and although she was out of breath she went straight to their door and burst in.

'What do you mean by this?' she began, turning on the centre light, only to find that Gloria and Bea were fast asleep. Or were they? She stood for a minute to make sure they were not pretending, but they were in a deep sleep. They hadn't even stirred when she'd opened the door so roughly and put on the light. She turned the light off gently, closed the door, and went out. Not a whit less angry though, she made for her own room – the room she shared with Linda. There, the light was still on, and although at first Linda tried hard to pretend that she too was asleep, when Vera went over to the bed the child sat up with a scared look.

'Don't be cross, Mother,' she said. When Vera didn't answer she snuggled down. 'Linda sleepy,' she said coaxingly. 'Linda is going to sleep now.' When Vera still said nothing the child sat up again and reached out her arms. 'I'm sorry, Mother. I promise I won't get out of bed anymore. You can go down again.'

Vera was so tired she felt like leaving it at that, but curiosity got the better of her.

'Where were you? Who were you talking to?' It annoyed her to think that anyone, at that hour of night, should have encouraged the child to stay up.

'I was only saying goodnight,' Linda said.

'To whom?'

There was a slight pause.

'To Peggy!'

'Oh, is *that* so?' Vera couldn't keep the sarcasm out of her voice. Child though Linda was, and her own daughter at that, Vera despised her for using a sick girl as a cover for her own misconduct. 'You know

Peggy's trouble is that she cannot – *will not* – talk – how dare you tell me a lie.'

Linda's eyes opened wide with surprise and indignation. 'She talked to *me*!'

Vera felt herself trembling with fury, but now Linda too was furious. 'I don't tell lies. I talk to her every evening – I go in and say goodnight to her.'

Vera suddenly thought she saw a chance to save face for both of them.

'You have been very naughty, Linda,' she said, 'but I will forgive you because perhaps you didn't mean to tell a lie – not a real lie anyway – you may have spoken to Peggy, but that's very different from saying Peggy spoke to you. That's what I thought you meant. Go to sleep now like a good child and we'll talk about it in the morning.' In the morning she would question her more closely and find out how the sick girl had reacted. To her surprise, she saw that Linda's eyes were blazing.

'But she *did* talk to me – she did!' the child cried. 'Last night and the night before when you went downstairs I went to her door and said goodnight to her, and *she* said goodnight to me.'

Vera stared. 'But, Linda, why, when she wouldn't speak to her mother, or to the doctor, or Father Tom, or anyone, why, *why* should she talk to *you*?'

'She likes me, that's why!' Linda flashed. 'She told me so.' Her indignation was so convincing Vera was nearly persuaded she was telling the truth until she remembered something.

'I'm sorry, Linda,' she said coldly, 'but I happen to know Peggy's mother sleeps in the same room with her. It's funny her mother didn't hear her talking!'

'I know her mother sleeps there,' Linda said, 'but I listen until she goes out to the bathroom to brush her teeth.'

'And how long does that take?' It was bad enough that one's child should be a liar without finding she was a highly accomplished one. 'Tonight you were laughing so loud I heard you downstairs, and – '

'Ah, but tonight was different,' Linda said, and she wriggled at the thought of the fun she'd had. 'Her mother fell asleep tonight, sitting in her chair. I heard her snoring; that's why I went in, and that's why we were laughing so loud – we were laughing at her mother going honk-honk.'

Even without Linda's imitation, Vera was begining to be convinced. She remembered the snores she'd heard as she came along the corridor. Linda leaned forward and cuddled against her.

'Linda wouldn't tell a lie,' she said smugly.

'I know that, darling,' Vera had to say, but she was too exhausted for any more discussion. She put the child back and pulled up the bedclothes. Should she go down again and tell all this to Father Tom? she wondered. 'Just a minute, Linda.' She went out into the corridor and tiptoed to the door of the sick girl's room. There was no light under the door, but yes, it was from there the snores were coming, and they were not the snores of a young girl, well or sick. That poor mother, she thought. She must be worn out. Was she still sitting up in her chair? This seemed an added reason to go down and tell Father Tom. On the other hand, was she really convinced that Linda had told the *whole* truth? Better not start a scare. Better leave it till morning. Before she went back to her room she looked over the bannisters and as far as she could see the lights were out below. When she went back Linda was fast asleep. Vera stood looking down at the child for a minute before she undressed and got into bed. She put out the light. In an instant she too was asleep.

When Vera woke she realised with a start that she had not heard the big Mass bell, much less the little bell for breakfast. And they were to have made an early start. Assisi was a good distance from Florence. She looked across at Linda's bed, but Linda had already gone down. The child's pyjamas and dressing-gown were thrown on the bed, and the wardrobe door hung open.

Springing up Vera opened the door and peeped along the corridor. Every door was open except one. And she could tell by the sounds from below that breakfast was well under way. A few minutes later, when she was dressed and about to hurry down the stairs herself, she paused and looked with curiosity at the one closed door. No sound came from the room – no sound whatever. Linda must have made up that story, she thought. In the daylight this didn't seem such a heinous offence for an imaginative child. Putting it out of her mind she ran down the stairs.

As an early start had been planned, everyone had come to breakfast dressed for the outing. Father Tom who was just tossing down the dregs of his last cup of coffee stood up.

'I thought you weren't coming,' he said, sitting down again and reaching for the coffee pot. 'This is still hot, and there's some toast left. You won't have time for a full breakfast, but we can make our first stop a bit earlier than usual.'

'I'd have sent word if I wasn't coming,' Vera said.

Father Tom looked sharply at her. 'I thought when Linda wasn't going you wouldn't be able to go either.'

Linda? Vera looked around the room. Linda was still at the table, and whereas Gloria and Bea were ready for the day, with their cardigans on, she was still in her slippers.

'Linda – why aren't you ready?' she called out.

Linda got up and ran over to her. 'Oh Mother, I can't go,' she said. She threw her arm around Vera, and at the same time she gave Father Tom an apologetic look. '*She* asked me not to go! Oh please, Mother. She's so lonely up there all day when everyone is gone off in the coach – except her mother. And her mother just sits and *cries*. Now that we've had such fun together she doesn't want me to go off all day too – oh *please*, Mother?'

Vera didn't need to ask who it was whom Linda meant. But Father Tom was mystified.

'What's all this?'

'Oh Father Tom, I should have told you last night,' Vera said contritely, 'but I didn't really believe Linda when she told me,' she added, trying not to see the hurt look on Linda's face. Reaching out she caught hold of Linda and almost shook her. 'I'm not completely sure that I do now either. *Linda*, are you making this up, because – ?'

Without being told any more, Father Tom understood.

'It's Peggy!' he said, and brushing Vera aside he knelt and put his hands on the child's shoulders. 'Did you see her this morning, Linda? Did she talk to you again?'

Linda's eyes lit up. Someone believed her. She threw her arms around Father Tom's neck.

'I don't want to stay at home,' she said. 'I want to go in the coach – but she *asked* me to stay.' The child's dilemma was clear, and it made the truth of her story clear too.

'I should have come down again last night and told you, Father, but – as I say – I didn't really believe her,' Vera repeated. 'What will you do?'

Sensing that something was wrong, Leo had come back into the dining-hall. The rest were filing into the sunlight through the door that Sister Patrick held open. Outside the coach was waiting.

'Get them all into the coach, Leo,' the priest said crisply.

'Can I do anything?' Vera asked humbly.

'Yes,' he said. 'Where is the girl's mother?' He looked around. Most times the mother had her meals on a tray in her daughter's room, but if she got a chance she slipped down to the dining-hall, ate it quickly and went right up again immediately.

'She was here when I came in,' Vera said, 'but I think she must have gone upstairs again.'

'Would you mind going up and telling her that I want her to come down. Don't tell her anything else. Just say I want her. Quickly!' Then he turned to Linda. 'I want *you* to go up and get your outdoor shoes and your cardigan and whatever else you want to take with you to Assisi – you must trust me, Linda,' he said, when the child started to protest. 'You're a big girl now, and I know that I can talk to you like a grown-up. Peggy has been very sick. That's why your mother was cross with you last night. But I think

Peggy may be getting better – that *you* may have made her better. And if she's better she can come to Assisi with you instead of you both staying at home!' In a quite different voice he pointed up the stairs. 'Go on now – go up, and when you've got your shoes and your cardigan go into Peggy's room and ask her to come with you. Wait there while she's dressing and come down with her. We'll be waiting for you in the coach.'

When a few minutes afterwards Vera came down accompanied by the girl's mother, Father Tom indicated to her that they were to go out to the coach. Vera's heart ached to see how docile pain and suffering had made the woman. When Vera took her arm she went with her without questioning.

Father Tom came out a minute later and joined them. He put his hand on the mother's arm. 'I think everything is going to be all right,' he said. Then he turned to the rest of the party. 'Take your places in the coach,' he ordered.

When they had all filed into the coach except for the sound of the motor that was now running there was a strange silence over the little group. Then, suddenly, as on the previous night, a peal of laughter came from inside the convent. It takes a great brightness to be brighter than the light of day, but that was how the laughter seemed to Vera.

'Is it Linda?' Father Tom asked, turning to her.

Almost afraid to speak, Vera shook her head. 'It's Peggy,' she said.

Then they heard footsteps coming down the stairs, young steps, silly steps, steps that stopped and skipped, skipped and stopped. The next minute the two young people ran out into the sunlight.

'Peggy!' the girl's mother whispered.

From the windows of the coach the others gaped.

'Hello, Mummy,' Peggy said. 'Hello, Father Tom.'

But Linda ran over to the priest. 'Can Peggy and I sit up in front with Luigi?' she asked, knowing well it was the seat of honour. When he nodded the two girls scrambled up into the coach.

'Peggy – Peggy, Peggy – ' Everyone wanted to say hello to her.

'Hello, everybody,' Peggy said and waved back to them from the front seat.

Father Tom took the mother by the arm.

'I told you everything would be all right, didn't I?' he said gently. 'Just take things easily now. Let her sit up front with Linda and Luigi, and forget the accident ever happened.'

Silently Vera handed Leo the woman's coat and handbag as Father Tom helped her into the bus and he and Leo got in after her.

Vera looked at Father Tom. Had he forgotten that now there would not be a seat for her?

'I'll stay behind, Father. Don't worry about me,' she said.

He had not forgotten. Practical to the last!

'And you have to pack for tomorrow!' he said, and as the coach started to move off he smiled at her.

L

A Memory

James did all right for a man on his own. An old
woman from the village came in for a few hours a day
and gave him a hot meal before she went home. She
also got ready an evening meal needing only to be
heated up. As well, she put his breakfast egg in a
saucepan of water beside the paraffin stove, with a box
of matches beside it in case he mislaid his own. She took
care of all but one of the menial jobs of living. The one
she couldn't do for him was one James hated most –
cleaning out ashes from the grate in his study and lighting up the new fire for the day.

James was an early riser and firmly believed in giving
the best of his brain to his work. So, the minute he was
dressed he went out to the kitchen and lit the stove
under the coffee pot. Then he got the ash bucket and
went at the grate. When the ashes were out the rest
wasn't too bad. There was kindling in the hot press and
the old woman left a few split logs for getting up a
quick blaze. He had the room well warmed by the time
he had eaten his breakfast. His main objection to doing
the grate was that he got his suit covered with ashes.
He knew he ought to wear tweeds now that he was
living full-time at the cottage, but he stuck obstinately
to his dark suit and white collar, feeling as committed
to this attire as to his single state. Both were part and

parcel of his academic dedication. His work filled his life as it filled his day. He seldom had occasion to go up to the University. When he went up it was to see Myra, and then only on impulse if for some reason work went against him. This did happen periodically in spite of his devotion to it. Without warning a day would come when he'd wake up in a queer, unsettled mood that would send him prowling around the cottage, lighting up cigarette after cigarette and looking out of the window until he'd have to face the fact that he was not going to do a stroke. Inevitably the afternoon would see him with his hat and coat on, going down the road to catch the bus for Dublin – and an evening with Myra.

This morning he was in fine fettle though, when he dug the shovel into the mound of grey ash. But he was annoyed to see a volley of sparks go up the black chimney. The hearth would be hot, and the paper would catch fire before he'd have time to build his little pyre. There was more kindling in the kitchen press, but he'd have felt guilty using more than the allotted amount, thinking of the poor old creature wielding that heavy axe. He really ought to split those logs himself.

When he first got the cottage he used to enjoy that kind of thing. But after he'd been made a research professor and able to live down there all year round he came to have less and less zest for manual work. He sort of lost the knack of it. Ah well, his energies were totally expended in mental work. It would not be surprising if muscularly he got a bit soft.

James got up off his knees and brushed himself down. The fire was taking hold. The nimble flames played in and out through the dead twigs as sunlight must once have done when the sap was green. Standing watching them, James flexed his fingers. He wouldn't like to think he was no longer fit. Could his increasing aversion to physical labour be a sign of decreasing vigour? He frowned. He would not consider himself a vain man, it was simply that he'd got used to the look of himself; was accustomed to his slight, spare figure. But surely by mental activity he burned up as much fuel as any navvy or stevedore? Lunatics never had to worry about exercise either! Who ever saw a corpulent madman? He smiled. He must remember to tell that to Myra. Her laugh was always so quick and responsive although even if a second or two later she might seize on some inherently serious point in what had at first amused her. It was Myra who had first drawn his attention to this curious transference – this drawing off of energies – from the body to the brain. She herself had lost a lot of the skill in her fingers. When she was younger – or so she claimed – she'd been quite a good cook, and could sew, and that kind of thing, although frankly James couldn't imagine her being much good about the house. But when she gave up teaching and went into free-lance translation her work began to make heavy demands on her, and she too, like him, lost all inclination for physical chores. Now – or so she said – she could not bake a cake to save her life. As for sewing – well here again frankly – to him the sight of a needle in her hand would be ludicrous. In fact he knew – they both knew – that when they first met, it was her lack of domesticity that had been the essence of her appeal for him. For a woman, it was quite remarkable how strong was the intellectual climate of thought in which she lived. She had concocted a sort of cocoon of thought and wrapped herself up in it. One became aware of it immediately one stepped inside her little flat. There was another thing! The way she used the word flat to designate what was really a charming little mews house. It was behind one of the Georgian squares, and it had a beautiful little garden at the back and courtyard in front. He hadn't been calling there for very long until he understood why she referred to it as her flat. It was a word that did not have unpleasant connotations of domesticity.

Her little place had a marvellously masculine air, and yet, miraculously, Myra herself remained very feminine. She was, of course, a pretty woman, although she hated him to say this – and she didn't smoke, or drink more than a dutiful pre-dinner sherry with him, which she often forgot to finish. And there was a nice scent from her clothes, a scent at times quite disturbing. It often bothered him, and was occasionally the cause of giving her the victory in one of the really brilliant arguments that erupted so spontaneously the moment he stepped inside the door.

Yes, it was hard to believe Myra could ever have been a home-body. But if she said it was so, then it *was* so. Truth could have been her second name. With regard to her domestic failure, she had recently told him a most amusing story. He couldn't recall the actual incident, but it had certainly corroborated her theory of the transference of skill. It was – she said – as if part of her had become palsied, although at the time her choice of that word had made him wince, it was so altogether unsuitable for a woman like her, obviously now in her real prime. He'd pulled her up on that. Verbal exactitude was something they both knew to be of the utmost importance, although admittedly rarer to find in a woman than a man.

'It is a quality I'd never have looked to find in a woman, Myra,' he'd said to her on one of his first visits to the flat – perhaps his very first.

He never forgot her answer.

'It's not something I'd ever expect a man to look for in a woman,' she said. 'Thank you, James, for not jumping to the conclusion that I could not possibly possess it.'

Yes – that must have been on his first visit because he'd been startled by such quick-fire volley in reply to what had been only a casual compliment. No wonder their friendship got off to a flying start!

Thinking of the solid phalanx of years that had been built up since that evening, James felt a glow of satisfaction, and for a moment he didn't realise that the fire he was supposed to be tending had got off to a good start, and part at least of his sense of well-being was coming from its warmth stealing over him.

The flames were going up the chimney with soft nervous rushes and the edges of the logs were deckled with small sharp flames, like the teeth of a saw. He could safely leave it now and have breakfast. But just then he did remember what it was Myra had been good at when she was young. Embroidery! She had once made herself an evening dress with the bodice embroidered all over in beads. And she'd worn it! So it must have been well made. Even his sister Kay, who disliked Myra, had to concede she dressed well. Yes, she must indeed have been fairly good at sewing in her young days. Yet one day recently when she ripped her skirt in the National Library she hadn't been able to mend it.

'It wasn't funny, James,' she chided when he laughed. 'The whole front pleat was ripped. I had to borrow a needle and thread from the lavatory attendant. Fortunately I had plenty of time – so when I'd taken it off and sewed it up I decided to give it a professional touch – a finish – with a tailor's arrow. It took time but it was well done and the lavatory attendant was very impressed when I held the skirt up! But next minute when I tried to step into it I found I'd sewn the back to the front. I'd formed a sort of gusset. Can you picture it. I'd turned it into trousers!'

Poor Myra! He laughed still more.

'I tell you, it's not funny, James. And it's the same with cooking. I used at least to be able to boil an egg, whereas now – ' she shrugged her shoulders. 'You know how useless I am in the kitchen.'

She had certainly never attempted to cook a meal for him. They always went out to eat. There was a small café near the flat and they ate there. Or at least they did at the start. But when one evening they decided they didn't really want to go out – perhaps he'd had a headache, or perhaps it was a really wet night, but anyway whatever it was, Myra made no effort to – as she put it – slop up some unappetising smather. Instead she lifted the phone, and got on to the proprietor of their little café and – as she put it – administered such a dose of coaxy-orum – she really had very amusing ways of expressing herself – that he sent around two trays of food. Two trays, mind you. That was so like her – so quick, so clever. And tactful, too. That night marked a new stage in their relationship.

They'd been seeing a lot of each other by then. He'd been calling to the flat pretty frequently and when they went out for a meal, although the little café was always nearly empty, he had naturally paid the bill each time.

'We couldn't go on like that though, James!' she'd said firmly when he'd tried to pay for the trays of food that night. And she did finally succeed in making him see that if he were to come to the flat as often as she hoped he would – and as he himself certainly hoped – it would put her under too great an obligation to have him pay for the food every time.

'Another woman would be able to run up some tasty little dish that wouldn't cost tuppence,' she said, 'but –' she made a face '– that's out. All the same I can't let you put me under too great a compliment to you. Not every time.'

In the end they'd settled on a good compromise. They each paid for a tray.

He had had misgivings, but she rid him of them.

'What would you eat if I wasn't here, Myra?' he'd asked.

'I wouldn't have *cooked* anything, that's certain,' she said, and he didn't pursue the topic, permitting himself just one other brief enquiry.

'What do other people do, I wonder?'

This Myra dismissed with a deprecating laugh.

'I'm afraid I don't know,' she said. 'Or care! Do you?'

'Oh Myra!' In that moment he felt she elevated them both to such pure heights of integrity. 'You know I don't,' he said, and he'd laid his hand over hers as she sat beside him on the sofa.

'That makes two of us!' she said, and she drew a deep breath of contentment.

It was a rich moment. It was probably at that moment he first realised the uniquely undemanding quality of her feeling for him.

But now James saw that the fire was blazing madly. He had to put on another log or it would burn out too fast. He threw on a log and was about to leave the study when, as he passed his desk, a nervous impulse made him look to see that his papers were not disarranged, although there was no one to disturb them.

The papers, of course, were as he had left them. But then the same diabolical nervousness made him go over and pick up the manuscript. Why? He couldn't explain, except that he'd worked late the previous night and, when he did that, he was always idiotically nervous next day, as if he half expected to find the words had been mysteriously erased during the night. That had happened once! He'd got up one morning as usual, full of eagerness to take up where he thought he'd left off only to find he'd stopped in the middle of a sentence – had gone to bed defeated, leaving a most involved and complicated sentence unfinished. He'd only dreamed that he'd finished it off.

This morning, thank heavens, it was no dream. He'd finished the sentence – the whole chapter. It was the last chapter too. A little rephrasing, perhaps some rewording, and the whole thing would be ready for the typist.

Standing in the warm study with the pages of his manuscript in his hand James was further warmed by a self-congratulatory glow. This was the most ambitious thing he'd attempted so far – it was no less than an effort to trace the creative process itself back, as it were, to its source-bed. How glad he was that he'd stuck at it last night. He'd paid heavily for it by tossing around in the sheets until nearly morning. But it was worth it. His intuitions had never yielded up their meanings so fast or so easily. But suddenly his nervousness returned. He hoped to God his writing wasn't illegible? No. It was readable. And although his eye did not immediately pick up any of the particularly lucid – even felicitous – phrases that he vaguely remembered having hit upon, he'd come on them later when he was re-reading more carefully.

Pleased, James was putting down the manuscript, but on an impulse he took up the last section again. He'd bring it out to the kitchen and begin his re-reading of it while he was having his breakfast, something he never did, having a horror of foodstains on paper. It might, as it were, recharge his batteries, because in spite of his satisfaction with the way the work was going, he had to admit to a certain amount of physical lethargy, due to having gone to bed so late.

It was probably wiser in the long run to do like Myra and confine oneself to a fixed amount of work per day. Nothing would induce Myra to go beyond her pre-determined limit of two thousand words a day. Even when things were going well! It was when they were going well that paradoxically she often stopped work. Really her method of working amazed him. When she encountered difficulty she went doggedly on, worrying at a word like a dog with a bone – as she put it – in order, she explained, to avoid carrying over her frustration with it to the next day. On the other hand, when things were going well and her mind was leaping forward like a flat stone skimming the surface of a lake (her image again, not his, but good, good) *then* sometimes she stopped.

'Because then, James, I have a residue of enthusiasm to start me off next day! I'm not really a dedicated scholar like you – I need stimulus.'

She had a point. But her method wouldn't work for him. It would be mental suicide for him to tear himself away when he was excited. It was only when things got sticky he stopped. When an idea sort of seized up in his mind and he couldn't go on.

There was nothing sticky about last night though. Last night his brain buzzed with ideas. Yet now, sitting down to his egg, the page in his hand seemed oddly dull – a great hunk of abstraction. He took the top off the egg before reading on. But after a few paragraphs he looked at the numbering of the pages. Had the pages got mixed up? Here was a sentence that seemed to be in the wrong place. The whole passage made no impact. And what was this? He'd come on a line that was meaningless, absolutely meaningless – gibberish. With a sickening feeling James put down the manuscript and took a gulp of coffee. Then, by concentrating hard he could perceive – could at least form a vague idea of – what he'd been trying to get at in this clumsy passage. At one point indeed he had more or less got it, but the chapter as a whole – ? He sat there stunned.

What had happened? Could it be that what he'd taken for creative intensity had been only nervous exhaustion? Was that it? Was Myra right? Should he have stopped earlier? Out of the question. In the excited state he'd been in, he wouldn't have slept a wink at all – even in the early hours. And what else could he have done but go to bed? A walk, perhaps? At that time of night? On a country road in the pitch dark? It was all very well for Myra – the city streets were full of people at all hours, brightly lit, and safe underfoot.

Anyway Myra probably did most of her work in the morning. He didn't really know for sure of course, except that whenever he turned up at the flat there was never any sign of papers about the place. The thought of that neat and orderly flat made him look around the cottage and suddenly he felt depressed. The old woman did her best, but she wasn't up to very much. The place could do with a rub of paint, the woodwork at least, but he certainly wasn't going to do it. He wouldn't be able. James frowned again. Why was his mind harping on this theme of fitness? He straightened up as if in protest at some accusation, but almost at once he slumped down, not caring.

He got exercise enough on the days he went to Dublin. First the walk to the bus. Then the walk at the other end, because no matter what the weather, he always walked from the bus to the flat. It was a good distance too, but it prolonged his anticipation of the evening ahead.

Ah well! He wouldn't be going today. That was certain. He gathered up his pages. He'd have to slog at this thing till he got it right. He swallowed down the last of his coffee. Back to work.

The fire at any rate was going well. It was roaring up the chimney. The sun too was pouring into the room. Away across the river in a far field cattle were lying down: a sign of good weather it was said.

Hastily, James stepped back from the window and

sat down at his desk. It augured badly for his work when he was aware of the weather. Normally he couldn't have told if the day was wet or fine.

That was the odd thing about Dublin. There, the weather did matter. There he was aware of every fickle change in the sky, especially on a day like today that began with rain and later gave way to sunshine. The changes came so quick in the city. They took one by surprise, although one was alerted by a thousand small signs, whereas the sodden fields were slow to recover after the smallest shower. In Dublin the instant there was a break in the clouds, the pavements gave back an answering glint. And after that came a strange white light mingling water and sun, a light that could be perceived in the reflections under foot without raising one's eyes to the sky at all. And how fast then the paving stones dried out into pale patches. Like stepping stones, these patches acted strangely on him, putting a skip into his otherwise sober step!

Talk of the poetry of Spring. The earth's rebirth! Where was it more intoxicating than in the city, the cheeky city birds filling the air with song, and green buds breaking out on branches so black with grime it was as if iron bars had sprouted. Thinking of the city streets his feet ached to be pacing them. James glanced out again at the fields with hatred.

Damn, damn, damn. The damage was done. He'd let himself get unsettled. It would be Dublin for him today. He looked at the clock. He might even go on the early bus. Only what would he do up there all day? His interest in Dublin had dwindled to its core, and the core was Myra.

All the same, he decided to go on the early bus. 'Come on, James! Be a gay dog for once. Get the early bus. You'll find plenty to do. The bookshops! The National Library! Maybe a film? Come on. You're going whether you like it or not, old fellow.'

Catching up the poker James turned the blazing logs over to smother their flames. A pity he'd lit the fire, or rather it was a pity it couldn't be kept in till he got back. It would be nice to return to a warm house. But old Mrs Nully had a mortal dread of the cottage taking fire in his absence. James smiled thinking how she had recently asked why he didn't install central heating. In a three-roomed cottage! Now where on earth had she got that notion he wondered, as he closed the door and put the key under the mat for her. Then, as he strode off down to the road, he remembered that a son of hers had been taken on as houseman in Asigh House, and the son's wife gave a hand there at weekends. The old woman had probably been shown over the house by them before the Balfes moved into it.

The Balfes! James was nearly at the road, and involuntarily he glanced back across the river to where a fringe of fir trees in the distance marked out the small estate of Asigh. Strange to think – laughable really – that Emmy, who once had filled every cranny of his mind, should only come to mind now in a train of thought that had its starting point in a plumbing appliance!

Here James called himself to order. It was a gross exaggeration to have said – even to himself – that Emmy had ever entirely filled his mind. He'd only known her for a year, and that was the year he finished his Ph.D. He submitted the thesis at the end of the year, and his marks, plus the winning of the travelling scholarship, surely spoke for a certain detachment of mind even when he was most obsessed by her?

He glanced back again at the far trees. Emmy only stood out in his life because of the violence of his feeling for her. It was something he had never permitted himself before; and never would again. When the affair ended, it ended as completely as if she had been a little skiff upon a swiftly flowing river, which, when he'd cut the painter, was carried instantly away. For a time he'd had no way of knowing whether it had capsized or foundered. As it happened, Emmy had righted herself and come to no harm.

Again, James had to call himself to order. How cruel he made himself seem by that metaphor. Yet for years that was how he'd felt obliged to put it to himself. That was how he'd put it to Myra when he first told her about Emmy. But Myra was quick to defend him, quick to see, and quick to show him how he had acted in self-defence. His career would have been wrecked, because of course with a girl like Emmy marriage would have become inescapable. And, of course, then as now, marriage for him was out. It was never really in the picture.

Later, after Myra appeared on the scene, he came to believe that a man and woman could enter into a marriage of minds.

'But when one is young, James,' Myra said, 'one can't be expected to be both wise and foolish at the same time.'

A good saying. He'd noticed, and appreciated, the little sigh with which she accompanied her words, as if she didn't just feel *for* him but *with* him.

Then she asked the question that a man might have asked.

'She married eventually I take it, this Emmy?'

'Oh good lord, yes.' How happy he was to be able to answer in the affirmative. If Emmy had not married it would have worried him all his life. But she did. And, all things considered, surprisingly soon.

'Young enough to have a family?' Myra probed, but kindly, kindly. He nodded. 'I take it,' she said then, more easily, 'I take it she married that student who –'

James interrupted ' – the one she was knocking around with when I first noticed her?'

'Yes, the one that was wrestling with that window when you had to step down from the rostrum and yank it open yourself?'

Really Myra was unique. Her grasp of the smallest details of that incident, even then so far back in time, was very gratifying.

He had been conducting a tutorial and the lecture room got so stuffy he'd asked if someone would open a window? But when a big burly fellow – the footballer type – tried with no success, James strode down the classroom himself, irritably, because he half thought the fellow might be having him on to create a diversion. And when he had to lean in across a student whose chair was right under the window, he was hardly aware it was a girl, as he exerted all his strength to bring down the heavy sash. Only when the sash came down and the fresh air rushed in overhead did he find he was looking straight into the eyes of a girl – Emmy.

That was all. But during the rest of the class their eyes kept meeting. And the next day it was the same.

Then he began to notice her everywhere, in the corridors, in the Main Hall, and once across the Aula Maxima at an inaugural ceremony. And she'd seen him too. He knew it. But for a long time, several weeks, there was nothing between them except this game of catch-catch with their eyes. And always, no matter how far apart they were, it was as if they had touched.

James soon found himself trembling all over when her eyes touched him. Then one day in the library she passed by his desk and he saw that a paper in her hand was shaking as if there was a breeze in the air. But there was no breeze. Still, deliberately, he delayed the moment of speaking to her because there was a kind of joy in waiting. And funnily enough when they did finally speak neither of them could afterwards remember what their first spoken words had been. They had already said so much with their eyes.

Myra's comment on this, though, was very shrewd. 'You had probably said all there was to say, James.' Again she gave that small sigh of hers that seemed to put things in proportion: to place him, and Emmy too, on the map of disenchantment where all mankind, it seems, must sojourn for a time. And indeed it was sad to think that out of the hundreds of hours that he and Emmy had spent together, wandering along the damp paths of Stephen's Green, sitting in little cafés, and standing under the lamps of Leeson Street where he was in lodgings, he could recall nothing of what was said. 'You probably spent most evenings trying out ideas for your thesis on her, poor girl.' Myra had a dry humour at times, but he had to acknowledge it was likely enough, although if so, Emmy used to listen as if she were drinking in every word.

M

When he'd got down at last to the actual writing of the thesis they did not meet so often. In fact he could never quite remember their last meeting either. Not even what they had said to each other at parting. Of course long before that they must have faced up to his situation. He'd been pretty sure of getting the travelling scholarship, so it must have been an understood thing that he'd be going away for at least two years. And in the end, he left a month sooner than he'd intended. They never actually did say good-bye. He'd gone without seeing her – just left a note at her digs. And for a while he wasn't even sure if she'd got it. She'd got it all right. She wrote and thanked him. How that smarted! *Thanked* him for breaking it off with her. Years later, telling Myra, he still felt the sting of that.

Myra was marvellous though.

'Hurt pride, my dear James. Nothing more, don't let it spoil what is probably the sweetest thing in life – for all of us, men or women – our first shy, timid love.' There was a tenderness in her voice. Was she remembering some girlish experience of her own? The pang of jealousy that went through him showed how little Emmy had come to mean to him.

Myra put him at ease.

'We all go through it, James, it's only puppy love.'

'Puppy love! I was twenty-six, Myra!'

'Dear, dear James.' She smiled. 'Don't get huffy. I know quite well what age you were. You were completing your Ph.D., and you were old enough to conduct tutorials. You were not at the top of the tree, but you had begun the ascent!'

It was so exactly how he'd seen himself in those

days, that he laughed. And with that laugh the pain
went out of the past.

'Dear James,' she said again, 'anyone who knows
you – and loves you,' she added quickly, because they
tried never to skirt away from that word love, although
they gave it a connotation all their own, 'anyone who
loves you, James, would know that even then, where
women were concerned, you'd be nothing but a lanky,
bashful boy. Wait a minute!' She sprang up from the
sofa. 'I'll show you what I mean.' She took down the
studio photograph she'd made him get taken the day
of his honorary doctorate. 'Here!' She shoved the
silver frame into his hands, and going into the room
where she slept, she came back with another photograph. 'You didn't know I had this one?' He saw with
some chagrin that it was a blow-up from a group
photograph taken on the steps of his old school at the
end of his last year. 'See!' she said. 'It's the same face
in both, the same ascetical features, the same look of
dedication.' Then she pressed the frame end face in-
ward, against her breast. 'Oh James, I bet Emmy was
the first girl you ever looked at! My dear, it was not so
much the girl as the experience itself that bowled you
over.'

Emmy was not the first girl he'd looked at. In those
days he was always looking at girls, but looking at
them from an unbridgeable distance. When he looked
at Emmy the space between them seemed to be instantly obliterated. Emmy had felt the same. That day
in class her mind had been a million miles away. She
was trying to make up her mind about getting engaged
to the big burly fellow, the one who couldn't open the
window; James could not remember his name, but he

was a type that could be attractive to women. The fellow was pestering her to marry him, and the attentions of a fellow like that could have been very flattering to a girl like Emmy. She was so young. Yet, after she met *him* it was as if a fiery circle had been blazed around them, allowing no way out for either until he, James, in the end had to close his eyes and break through, not caring about the pain as long as he got outside again.

Because Myra was right. Marriage would have put an end to his academic career. For a man like him it would have been suffocating.

'Even now!' Myra said, and there was a humorous expression on her face, because of course, in their own way, he and Myra *were* married. Then, in a business-like way, as if she were filling up a form for filing away, she asked him another question. 'What family did they have?'

'She had five or six children, I think, although she must have been about thirty by the time she married,' James couldn't help throwing his eyes up to heaven at the thought of such a household. Myra too raised her eyebrows.

'You're joking?' she said. 'Good old Balfe!' But James was staring at her, hardly able to credit she had picked up Emmy's married name. He himself had hardly registered it, the first time *he'd* heard it, so that when last summer Asigh House had been bought by people named Balfe, it simply hadn't occurred to him that it could have been Emmy and her husband until one day on the road a car passed him and the woman beside the driver reminded him oddly of her. The woman in the car was softer and plumper and her hair was looser and more untidy – well fluffier anyway – than Emmy's used to be, or so he thought, until suddenly he realised it *was* her. Emmy! She didn't recognise him though. But then she wasn't looking his way. She was looking out over the countryside through which she was passing. It was only when the car turned left at the cross-road the thought hit him, that she had married a man named Balfe, and that Balfe was the name of the people who'd bought Asigh. It was a shock. Not only because of past associations, but more because he had never expected any invasion of his privacy down here. It was his retreat, from everything and everyone. Myra – even Myra – had never been down there. She was too sensible to suggest such a thing. And he wouldn't want her to come either.

Once when he'd fallen ill he'd lost his head and sent her a telegram, but even then she'd exercised extreme discrimination. She despatched a nurse to take care of him, arranging with the woman to phone her each evening from the village. Without once coming down, she had overseen his illness – which fortunately was not of long duration. She had of course ascertained to her satisfaction that his condition was not serious. The main thing was that she set a firm precedent for them both. It was different when he was convalescing. Then she insisted that he come up to town and stay in a small hotel near the flat, taking his evening meal with her, as on ordinary visits except – James smiled – except that she sent a taxi to fetch him, and carry him back, although the distance involved was negligible, only a block or two.

Remembering her concern for him on that occasion, James told himself that he could never thank her enough. He resolved to let her see he did not take her goodness for granted. Few women could be as self-effacing.

Yet, in all fairness to Emmy, she had certainly effaced herself fast. One might say drastically. After that one note of thanks – it jarred again that she had put it like that – he had never once heard or seen her until that day she passed him here on the road in her car. So much for his fears for his privacy. Unfounded! For days he'd half expected a courtesy call from them, but after a time he began to wonder if they were aware at all that he lived in the neighbourhood? After all, their property was three or four miles away, and the river ran between. It was just possible Emmy knew nothing of his existence. Yet somehow, he doubted it. As the crow flies he was less than two miles away. He could see their wood. And was it likely the local people would have made no mention of him? No, it was hard to escape the conclusion that Emmy might be avoiding him. Although Myra – who was never afraid of the truth – had not hesitated to say that Emmy might have forgotten him altogether!

'Somehow I find that hard to believe, Myra,' he'd said, although after he'd made the break, there had been nothing. Nothing, nothing, nothing.

But Myra was relentless.

'You may not like to believe it, James, but it could be true all the same,' she said. Then she tried to take the hurt out of her words by confessing that she herself found it dispiriting to think a relationship that had gone so deep, could be erased completely. 'I myself can't bear to think she did not recognise you that day she passed you on the road. *She* may have changed –

you said she'd got stouter – ' That wasn't the word he'd used, but he'd let it pass – 'whereas you, James, can hardly have changed at all, in essentials, I mean. Your figure must be the same as when you were a young man. I can't bear to think she didn't even *know* you.'

'She wasn't looking straight at me, Myra.'

'No matter! You'd think there'd have been some telepathy between you; some force that would *make* her turn. Oh, I can't bear it!'

She was so earnest he had to laugh.

'It is a good job she didn't see me,' he said. Emmy being nothing to him then, it was just as well there should be no threat to his peace and quiet.

Such peace; such quiet. James looked around at the sleepy countryside. The bus was very late though! What was keeping it?

Ah, here it came. Signalling to the driver, James stepped up quickly on to the running-board so the man had hardly to do more than go down into first gear before starting off again. In spite of how few passengers there were, the windows were fogged up and James had to clear a space on the glass with his hand to see out. It was always a pleasant run through the rich Meath fields, but soon the unruly countryside gave way to neatly squared-off fields with pens and wooden palings, where cattle were put in for the night before being driven to the slaughter-house.

James shuddered. He was no country-man. Not by nature anyway. He valued the country solely for the protection it gave him from people. When he lived in Dublin he used to work in the National Library, but as he got older he began to feel that in the eyes of the students and the desk-messengers, he could have appeared

eccentric. Not objectionably so, just rustling his papers
too much, and clearing his throat too loudly; that kind
of thing. He'd have been the first to find that annoying
in others when he was young. The cottage was much
better. It also served to put that little bit of distance
between him and Myra which they both agreed was
essential.

'If I lived in Dublin I'd be here at the flat every
night of the week,' he'd once said to her. 'I'm better
off down there – I suppose – stuck in the mud!'

That was an inaccurate – an unfair – description of
his little retreat, but the words had come involuntarily
to his lips which showed how he felt about the country
in general. The city streets of Dublin were so full of
life, and the people were so dapper and alert compared
with the slow-moving country people. Every time he
went up there he felt like an old fogy – that was until
he got to Myra's – because Myra immediately gave him
back a sense of being alive. Mentally at least Myra made
him feel more alive than twenty men.

The bus had now reached O'Connell Bridge, where
James usually descended, so he got out. He ought to
have got out sooner and walked along the Quays. One
could kill a whole morning looking over the book
barrows. Now he would have to walk back to them.

Perhaps he ought not to have come on the early bus?
It might not be so easy to pass the time. And after
browsing to his heart's content and leaning for a while
looking over the parapet on to the Liffey, it was still
only a little after 1 o'clock when he strolled back to the
centre of the city. He'd have to eat something and that
would use up another hour or more. He'd buy a paper
and sit on over his coffee.

James hadn't bargained on the lunchtime crowds though. All the popular places were crowded, and in a few of the better places, one look inside was enough to send him off! These places too were invaded by the lunchtime hordes, and the menu would cater for these barbarians. If there should by chance happen to be a continental dish on the menu – a goulash or a pasta – it would nauseate him to see the little clerks attacking it with knife and fork as if it was a mutton chop.

At this late hour how about missing out on lunch altogether? It never hurt to skip a meal, although, mind you, he was peckish. How about a film? He hadn't been in a cinema for years. And just then, as if to settle the matter – James saw he was passing a cinema. It was exceptionally small for a city cinema, but without another thought he bolted inside.

Once inside, he regretted that he hadn't checked the time of the showings. He didn't fancy sitting through a newsreel, to say nothing of a cartoon. He had come in just in the middle of a particularly silly cartoon. He sat in the dark fuming. To think he'd let himself in for this stuff. It was at least a quarter of an hour before he realised with rage that he must have strayed into one of the new-fangled newsreel cinemas about which Myra had told him. For another minute he sat staring at the screen, trying to credit the mentality of people who voluntarily subjected themselves to this kind of stuff. He was about to leave and make for the street, when without warning his eyes closed. He didn't know for how long he had dozed off, but on waking he was really ravenous. But wouldn't it be crazy to eat at this hour and spoil his appetite for the meal with Myra? He could, he supposed, go around to the flat earlier – now

– immediately? Why wait any longer? But he didn't know at what hour Myra herself got there. All he knew was that she was always there after seven, the time he normally arrived.

But wasn't it remarkable now he came to think of it, that she *was* always there when he called. Very occasionally at the start she had let drop dates on which she had to go to some meeting or other, and he'd made a mental note of them, but as time went on she gave up these time-wasting occupations. There had been one or two occasions she had been going out, but had cancelled her arrangements immediately he came on the scene. He had protested of course, but lamely, because quite frankly it would have been frightfully disappointing to have come so far and found she really had to go out.

Good God – supposing that were to happen now? James was so scared at the possibility of such a catastrophe he determined to lose no more time but get around there quick. Just in case. He stepped out briskly.

The lane at the back of Fitzwilliam Square, where Myra had her mews, was by day a hive of small enterprises. A smell of cellulosing and sounds of welding filled the air. In one courtyard there was a little fellow who dealt in scrap-iron and he made a great din. But by early evening, the big gates closed on these businesses, the high walls made the lane a very private place, and the mews-dwellers were disturbed by no sound harsher than the late song of the birds nesting in the trees of the doctors' gardens.

Walking down the lane and listening to those sleepy bird-notes gave James greater pleasure than walking on any country road. His feet echoed so loudly in the stillness that sometimes before he rapped on her gate at all, Myra would come running out across the court-yard to admit him. A good thing that! Because other-wise he'd have had to rap with his bare knuckles; Myra had no knocker.

'You know I don't encourage callers, James,' she'd said once smiling. 'Few people ferret me out here – except you; and, of course, the tradesmen. And I know their step too! It's nearly as quiet here as in your cottage.'

'Quiet?' He'd raised his eyebrows. 'Listen to those birds; I never heard such a din!'

Liking a compliment to be oblique, she'd squeezed his arm as she drew him inside.

This evening however James was less than halfway down the lane when at the other end he saw Myra appear at the wicket gate. If she hadn't been bare-headed he'd have thought she was going out!

'Myra?' he called in some dismay.

She laughed as she came to meet him. 'I heard your footsteps,' she said. 'I told you! I always do.'

'From this distance?'

She took his arm and smiled up at him. 'That's nothing! It's a wonder I don't hear you walking down the country road to get the bus.' She matched her step with his. Normally he hated to be linked, but with Myra it seemed to denote equality, not dependence. Suddenly she unlinked her arm. 'Well, I may as well confess something,' she said more seriously. 'This evening I was listening for you. I was expecting you.

They had reached the big wooden gate of the mews

and James, glancing in through the open wicket across the courtyard, was startled to see, through the enormous window by which she had replaced the doors of the coach-house, that the little table at which they ate was indeed set up, and with places laid for two! She wasn't joking then? An unpleasant thought crossed his mind – was she expecting someone else? But reading his mind, Myra shook her head.

'Only you, James.'

'I don't understand – '

'Neither do I!' she said quickly. 'I *was* expecting you though. And I ordered our trays!' Here she wrinkled her nose in a funny way she had. 'I made the order a bit more conservative than usual. No prawns!' He understood at once. He loved prawns. 'So you see,' she continued, 'if my oracle failed, and you didn't come, the food would do for sandwiches tomorrow. As you know, I'm no use at hotting up left-overs. It smacks too much of – '

He knew. He knew.

'Too wifey,' he smiled. And she smiled. This was the word they'd ear-marked to describe a certain type of woman they both abhorred.

'You could always have fed the prawns to the cat next door,' James said. 'Whenever I'm coming he's sitting on the wall smacking his lips.'

'But James,' she said, and suddenly she stopped smiling, 'he doesn't know when you're coming – any more than me!'

'Touché,' James admitted to being caught out there. He wasn't really good at smart remarks. 'Ah well, it's a lucky cat who knows there's an even chance of a few prawns once or twice a month. That's more than most cats can count on.' Bending his head he followed her in through the wicket. 'Some cats have to put up with a steady diet of shepherd's pie and meat loaf.'

They were inside now, and he sank down on the sofa. Myra, who was still standing, shuddered.

'What would I do if you were the kind of man who *did* like shepherd's pie?' she said. 'I'm sure there are such men.' But she couldn't keep up the silly chaff. 'I think maybe I'd love you enough to try and make it – ' she laughed, ' – if I could. I don't honestly think I'd be able. The main thing is that you are *not* that type. Let's stop fooling. Here, allow me to give you a kiss of gratitude – for being you.'

Lightly she laid her cheek against his, while he for his part took her hand and stroked it.

It was one of the more exquisite pleasures she gave him, the touch of her cool skin. His own hands had a tendency to get hot although he constantly wiped them with his handkerchief. He had always preferred being too cold to being too hot. Once or twice when he had a headache – which was not often – Myra had only to place her hand on his forehead for an instant and the throbbing ceased. This evening he didn't have a headache but all the same he liked the feel of her hand on his face.

'Do that again,' he said.

'How about fixing the drinks first?' she said.

That was his job. But he did not want to release her hand, and he made no attempt to stand up. Unfortunately just then there was a rap on the gate.

'Oh bother,' he said.

'It's only the Catering Service,' Myra said, and for a minute he didn't get the joke. She laughed then and he noticed she meant the grubby little pot-boy who brought the trays around from the café.

'Let me get them,' he said, but she had jumped up and in a minute she was back with them.

'I must tell you,' she said. 'You know the man who owns the café? Well, he gave me such a dressing-down this morning when I was ordering these.' James raised his eyebrows as he held open the door of the kitchenette to let her through. 'Just bring me the warming plate, will you please, James,' she said interrupting herself. 'I'll pop the food on it for a second while we have our little drink.' She glanced at her watch. 'Oh, it's quite early still.' She looked back at him. 'But you were a little later than usual, I think, weren't you?'

'I don't think so,' he said vaguely, as he fitted the plug of the food-warmer into the socket. 'If anything, I think I was a bit earlier. But I could be wrong. When one has time to kill it's odd how often one ends up being late in the end!'

'Time to kill?'

She looked puzzled. Then she seemed to understand. 'Oh James. You make me tired. You're so punctilious. Haven't I told you a thousand times that you don't have to be polite with me? If your bus got in early you should have come straight to the flat! Killing time indeed! Standing on ceremony, eh?'

He handed her her drink.

'You were telling me something about the proprietor of the café – that he was unpleasant about something? You weren't serious?'

'Oh that! Of course not.'

Yet for some reason he was uneasy. 'Tell me,' he said authoritatively.

Naturally, she complied. 'He was really very nice,' she said. 'He intended phoning me. He just wanted to say there was no need to wash the plates before sending them back. I'm to hand them to the messenger in the morning just as they are – and not *attempt* to wash them.' Knowing how fastidious she was, James was about to pooh-pooh the suggestion, but she forestalled him. 'I can wrap them up in the napkins, and then I won't be affronted by the sight. And I need feel under no compliment to the café – it's in their own interests as much as in mine. They have a big washing-machine – I've seen it – with a special compartment like a dentist's sterilisation cabinet, and of course they couldn't be sure that a customer would wash them properly. You can imagine the cat's lick some women would give them!'

James could well imagine it. He shuddered. Myra might hate housework, but anything she undertook she did to perfection. Unexpectedly she held out her glass.

'Let's have another drink,' she said. They seldom took more than one. 'Sit down,' she commanded. 'Let's be devils for once.' This time though she sat on the sofa and swung her feet up on it so he had to sit in the chair opposite. 'There's nothing that makes the ankles ache like thinking too hard,' she said.

James didn't really understand what she meant but he laughed happily.

'Seriously!' she said. 'I am feeling tired this evening. I'm so glad you came. I think maybe I worked extra hard this morning because I was looking forward to seeing you later. Oh, I'm so glad you came, James. I would have been bitterly disappointed if you hadn't showed up.'

James felt a return of his earlier uneasiness.

'I'm afraid that premonition of yours is more than I can understand,' he said, but he spoke patiently, because she was not a woman who had to be humoured. 'As a matter of fact I never had less intention of coming to town. I'd already lit the fire in my study when I suddenly took the notion. I had to put the fire out!'

At that, Myra left down her glass and swung her feet back on to the floor.

'What time did you leave?' she asked, and an unusually crisp note in her voice took him unawares.

'I thought I told you,' he said apologetically, although there was nothing for which to apologise. 'I came on the morning bus.'

'Oh!' It was only one word, but it fell oddly on his ears. She reached for her drink again then, and swallowed it down. Somehow that too bothered him. 'Is that what you meant by having to kill time?' she asked.

'Well – ' he began, not quite knowing what to say. He took up his own drink and let it down fairly fast for him.

'Oh, don't bother to explain,' she said. 'I think you will agree though it would have been a nice gesture to have lifted a phone and let me know you were in town and coming here tonight.'

'But – '

'No buts about it. You knew I'd be here waiting whether you came or not. Isn't that it?'

'Myra!'

He hardly recognised her in this new mood. Fortunately the next moment she was her old self again.

'Oh James, forgive me. It's just that you've *no* idea –

simply *no* idea – how much it meant to me tonight to know in advance – ' She stopped and carefully corrected herself ' – to have had that curious feeling – call it instinct if you like – that you were coming. It made such a difference to my whole day. But now – ' Her face clouded over, ' – to think that instead of just having had a hunch about it, I could have known for certain. Oh, if only you'd been more thoughtful, James.' Sitting up straighter she looked him squarely in the eye. 'Or were you going somewhere else and changed your mind?'

What a foolish question.

'As if I ever go anywhere else!'

Her face brightened a bit at that, but not much.

'You'll hardly believe it,' she said after a minute, 'but I could have forgiven you more easily if you had been going somewhere else, and coming here *was* an afterthought. It would have excused you more.'

Excused? What was all this about? He must have looked absolutely bewildered, because she pulled herself up.

'Oh James, please don't mind me.' She leant forward and laid a hand on his knee. 'Your visits give me such joy – I don't need to tell you that – I ought to be content with what I have. Not knowing in advance is one of the little deprivations that I just have to put up with, I suppose.'

But now James was beginning to object strongly to the way she was putting everything. He stood up. As if his doing so unnerved her, she stood up too.

'It may seem a small thing to ask from you, James, but I repeat what I said – you could have phoned me.' Then, as if that wasn't bad enough, she put it into the

N

future tense. 'If you would only try, once in a while, to give me a ring, even from the bus depot, so I could – '

' – could what?' James couldn't help the coldness in his voice, although considering the food that was ready on the food-warmer, his question, he knew, was ungenerous. On the other hand he felt it was absolutely necessary to keep himself detached, if the evening was not to be spoiled. He forced himself to speak sternly. 'Much as I enjoy our little meals together, it's not for the food I come here, Myra. You must know that.' He very, very nearly added that in any case he paid for his own tray, but when he looked at her he saw she had read these unsaid words from his eyes. He reddened. There was an awkward silence. Yet when she spoke she ignored everything he had said and harked back to what she herself had said.

'Wouldn't it be a very small sacrifice to make, James, when one thinks of all the sacrifices I've made for you? And over so many years?' Her words, which to him were exasperating beyond belief, seemed to drown her in a torrent of self-pity. 'So many, many years,' she whispered.

It was only ten.

'You'd think it was a lifetime,' he said irritably. Her face flushed.

'What is a lifetime, James?' she asked, and when he made no reply she helped him out. 'Remember it is not the same for a woman as for a man. *You* may think of yourself as a young blade, but I . . . '

She faltered again, as well she might, and bit her lip. She wasn't going to cry, was she? James was appalled. Nothing had ever before happened that could conceivably have given rise to tears, but it was an un-spoken law with them that a woman should never shed tears in public. Not just unspoken either. On one oc-casion years ago she herself had been quite explicit about it.

'We do cry sometimes, we women, poor weaklings that we are. But I hope I would never be foolish enough to cry in the presence of a man. And to do it to you of all people, James, would be despicable.' At the time he'd wondered why she singled him out. Did she think him more sensitive than most? He'd been about to ask when she'd given one of her witty twists to things. 'If I did, I'd have you snivelling too in no time,' she said.

Yet here she was now, for no reason at all, on the brink of tears, and apparently making no effort to fight them back.

Myra was making no effort to stem her tears because she did not know she was crying. She really did despise tears. But now it seemed to her that perhaps she'd been wrong in always hiding her feelings. Other women had the courage to cry. Even in public too. She'd seen them at parties. And recently she'd seen a woman walk-ing along the street in broad daylight with tears run-ning down her cheeks, not bothering to wipe them away. Thinking of such women, she wondered if she perhaps had sort of – she paused to find the right word – sort of denatured herself for James?

Denatured: it was an excellent word. She'd have liked to use it then and there but she had just enough sense left to keep it to herself for the moment. Some other time when they were talking about someone else, she would bring it out and impress him. She must not forget the word.

When Myra's thoughts returned to James she felt calmer about him. He was not unkind. He was not cruel – the opposite in fact. What had gone wrong this evening was more her fault than his. When they'd first met she had sensed deep down in him a capacity for the normal feelings of friendship and love. Yet throughout the years she had consistently deflected his feelings away from herself and consistently encouraged him to seal them off. Tonight it seemed that his emotional capacity was completely dried up. Despair overcame her. She'd never change him now. He was fixed in his faults, cemented into his barren way of life. Tears gushed into her eyes again but this time she leant her head back quickly to try and prevent them rolling down, but they brimmed over and splashed down on her hands.

'Oh James, I'm sorry,' she whispered, but she saw her apology was useless; the damage was done. Then her heart hardened. What harm? She wasn't really sorry. Not for him anyway. Oh, not for him. It was for herself she was sorry.

Grasping at a straw, then, she tried to tell herself, nothing was ever too late. Perhaps tonight some lucky star had stood still in the sky over her head and forced her to be true to herself for once. James would see the real woman for a change. Oh, surely he would? And surely he would come over and put his arm around her. He would: he would. She waited.

When he did not move, and did not utter a single word, she had to look up.

'Oh no!' she cried. For what she saw in his eyes was

ice. 'Oh James, have you no heart? What you have
done to me is unspeakable! Yet you can't even
pity me!'

James spoke at last. 'And what, Myra, what may I
ask, have I done to you?'

'You have – ' She stopped, and for one second she
thought she'd have control enough to bite back the
word, but she hadn't. 'You have denatured me,' she
said.

Oh God, what had she done *now*? Clapping her
hands over her mouth too late, she wondered if she
could pretend to some other meaning in the words. Instead, other words gushed out, words worse and more
hideous. Hearing them she herself could not understand where they came from. It was as if, out of the
corners of the room she was being prompted by the
voices of all the women in the world who'd ever been let
down, or fancied themselves badly treated. The room
vibrated with their whispers. Go on, they prompted.
Tell him what you think of him. Don't let him get
away with it. He has got off long enough. To stop the
voices she stuck her fingers into her ears, but the voices
only got louder. She had to shout them down. She saw
James's lips were moving, trying to say something,
but she could not hear him with all the shouting. When
she finally caught a word or two of what he said she
herself stopped trying to penetrate the noise. Silence
fell. She saw James go limp with relief.

'What did you say? I – I didn't hear you,' she
gulped.

'I said that if that's the way you feel, Myra, there's
nothing for me to do but to leave.'

She stared at him. He was going over to the clothes'

rack and was taking down his coat. What had got into them? How had they become involved in this vulgar scene? She had to stop him. If he went away like this would he ever come back? A man of his disposition? Could she take him back? Neither of them was of a kind to gloss over things and leave them unexplained knowing that unexplained they could erupt again – and again. Something had been brought to light that could never be forced back underground. Better all the same to let their happiness dry up if it must, than be blasted out of existence like this in one evening. Throwing out her arms she ran blindly towards him.

'James, I implore you. James! James! Don't let this happen to us.' She tried to enclose him with her arms, but somehow he evaded her and reached to take his gloves from the lid of the gramophone. Next thing she knew he'd be at the door.

'Do you realise what you're doing?' She pushed past him and ran to the door pressing her back against it, and throwing out her arms to either side. It was an outrageous gesture of crucifixion, and she knew she was acting out of character. She was making another and more frightful mistake. 'If you walk out this door, you'll never come through it again, James.'

All he did was try to push her to one side, not roughly, but not gently.

'James! Look at me!'

But what he said then was so humiliating she wanted to die.

'I am looking, Myra,' he said.

There seemed nothing left to do but hit him. She thumped at his chest with her closed fists. That made him stand back all right. She had achieved that at least! If she was not going to get a chance to undo the harm she'd done, then she'd go the whole hog and let him think the worst of her. She was ashamed to think she had been about to renege on herself. She flung out her arms again, not hysterically this time, but with passion, real, real passion. Let him see what he was up against. But whatever he thought, James said nothing. And he'd have to be the one to speak first. Myra couldn't trust herself any more.

In the end, she did have to speak. 'Say something, James,' she pleaded.

'All right,' he said then. 'Be so kind, Myra, as to tell me what you think you're gaining by this perform-ance?' he nodded at her outstretched arms. 'This nail-ing of yourself to the door like a stoat!'

The look in his eyes was ugly. She let her arms fall at once and running back to the sofa flung herself face down upon it screaming and kicking her feet.

She didn't even hear the door bang after him, or the gate slam.

Outside in the air James regretted that he had not shut the door more gently, but after the coarse and brutal words he had just used it was inconsistent to worry about the small niceties of the miserable busi-ness. His ugly words echoed in his mind, and he felt defiled by them. He had an impulse to go back and apologise, if only for his language. Nothing justified that kind of thing from a man. He actually raised his hand to rap on the gate, but he let it fall, overcome by a stronger impulse – to make good his escape. But as he hurried up the lane his unuttered words too seemed base and unworthy – a mean-minded figure of speech – that could only be condoned by the fact that he had been so grievously provoked, and by the overwhelming desire that had been engendered in him to get out in the air. If Myra had not stood aside and let him pass, he'd have used brute force. All the same nothing justified the inference that he was imprisoned. Never, never had she done anything to hold him. Never had he been made captive except perhaps by the pull of her mind upon his mind. He'd always been free to come or go as he chose. If in the flat they had become somewhat closed in of late it was from expediency – from not wanting to run into stupid people. If they had gone out to restaurants or cafés nowadays some fool would be sure to blunder over and join them, reducing their evening to the series of banalities that passed for conversation with most people. No, no, the flat was never a prison. Never. It was their nest. And now he'd fallen out of the nest. Or worse still been pushed out. All of a sudden James felt frightened. Was it possible she had meant what she said? Could it be that he would never again be able to go back there? Nonsense. She was hysterical.

He stood for a minute considering again whether he should not perhaps go back? Not that he'd relish it. But perhaps he ought to do so – in the interests of the future. No, he decided. Better give her time to calm down. Another evening would be preferable. If necessary he'd be prepared to come up again tomorrow evening. Or later this same evening? That would be more sensible. He looked back. She must be in a bad state when she hadn't run out after him. Normally she'd come to the gate and stay standing in the lane until he was out of sight. Even in the rain.

James shook his head. What a pity. If she'd come to the gate he could have raised his hands or something, given some sign – the merest indication would be enough – of his forgiveness. He could have let her see he bore no rancour. But the gesture would not want to be ambiguous. Not a wave; that would be over-cordial, and he didn't want her stumbling up the lane after him. No more fireworks thank you! But it would not want to appear final either. A raised hand would have been the best he could do at that time. He was going to walk on again when it occurred to him that if he'd gone back he need not have gone inside. Just a few words at the gate, but on the whole it was probably better to wait till she'd calmed down. Then he could safely take some of the blame, and help her to save face. Fortunately he did not have the vanity that, in another man, might make such a course impossible. It was good for the soul sometimes to assume blame – even wrongly. James immediately felt better, less bottled up. He walked on. But he could not rid his thoughts of the ugly business. He ought to have known that no woman on earth but was capable, at some time or another, of a lapse like Myra's. And Myra, of course, was a woman. How lacking he'd been in foresight. He'd have to go more carefully with her in future. Next time they met, although he would not try to exonerate himself from the part he'd played in the regrettable scene, at the same time it would not be right to rob her of the therapeutic effects of taking her share of the blame. He felt sure that, being fair-minded people, both of them, they would properly apportion the blame.

Anyway he resolved to put the whole thing out of

his mind until after he'd eaten. To think he'd eaten nothing since morning! After he'd had some food he'd be better able to handle the situation.

James had reached the other end of the lane now and gone out under the arch into Baggot Street again. Where would he eat? He'd better head towards the centre of the city. It ought not to be as difficult as it had been at midday, although an evening meal in town could be quite expensive. He didn't want a gala-type dinner, but not some awful slop either that would sicken him. He was feeling bad. The tension had upset his stomach and he was not sure whether he was experiencing hunger pangs or physical pain. Damn Myra. If she'd been spoiling for a fight, why the devil hadn't she waited till after their meal? She'd say this was more of his male selfishness, but if they had eaten they'd have been better balanced and might not have had a row at all. What a distasteful word – the word row! Yet, that's what it was – a common row. James came to a stand again. He wouldn't think twice of marching back and banging on the gate and telling her to stop her nonsense and put the food on the table. She was probably heartbroken. But if that was the case she'd have come to the door with her face flushed and her hair in disorder. Sobered by such a distasteful picture he walked on. He could not possibly subject her to humiliation like that. It would be his duty to protect her from exposing herself further. Perhaps he'd write her a note and post it in the late-fee box at the G.P.O. before he got the bus for home. She'd have it first thing in the morning, and after a good night's sleep she might be better able to take what he had to say. He began to compose the letter.

'*Dear Myra* – ' But he'd skip the beginning: that might be sticky. He'd have to give that careful thought. The rest was easy. Bits and pieces of sentences came readily to his mind – '*We must see to it that, like the accord that has always existed between us, discord too, if it should arise, must be* – '

That was the note to sound. He was beginning to feel his old self again. He probably ought to make reference to their next meeting? Not too soon – this to strike a cautionary note – but it might not be wise to let too much time pass either –

'*because, Myra, the most precious element of our friendship* – '

No, that didn't sound right. After tonight's scene, friendship didn't appear quite the right word. A new colouring had been given to their relationship by their tiff. But here James cursed under his breath. Tiff. Such a word! What next? Where were these trite words coming from? She'd rattled him all right. Damn it. Oh damn it.

James abandoned the letter for a moment when he realised he had been plunging along without regard to where he was headed. Where would he eat? There used to be a nice quiet little place in Molesworth Street, nearly opposite the National Library. It was always very crowded but with quite acceptable sorts from the library or the Arts School. He made off down Kildare Street.

When James reached the café in Molesworth Street however and saw the padlock on the area railings, he belatedly remembered it was just a coffee-shop, run by voluntary aid for some charitable organisation, and only open mornings. He stood, stupidly staring at the padlock. Where would he go now? He didn't feel like traipsing all over the city. Hadn't there been talk some time ago about starting a canteen in the National Library! Had that got under way? He looked across the street. An old gentleman was waddling in the Library gate with his brief case under his arm. James strode after him.

But just as he'd got to the entrance, the blasted porter slammed the big iron gate – almost in his face. He might have had his nose broken.

'Sorry, sir. The Library is closed. Summer holidays, sir.'

'But you just let in someone! I saw that man – '

James glared after the old man who was now ambling up the steps to the reading room.

'The gentleman had a pass, sir,' the porter said. 'There's a skeleton staff on duty in the stacks and the Director always gives out a few permits to people doing important research.' The fellow was more civil now. 'It's only fair, sir. It wouldn't do, sir, would it, to refuse people whose work is – ' But here he looked closer at James and, recognising him, his civility changed into servility. 'I beg your pardon, Professor,' he said. 'I didn't recognise you, sir. I would have thought you'd have applied for a permit. Oh dear, oh dear!' The man actually wrung his hands – 'if it was even yesterday, I could have got hold of the Director on the phone, but he's gone away – out of the country too I understand.'

'Oh, that's all right,' James said, somewhat mollified by being recognised and remembered. He was sorry that he, in turn, could not recall the porter's name. 'That's all right,' he repeated. 'I wasn't going to use the library anyway. I thought they might have opened that canteen they were talking about some time back – ?'

'Canteen, sir? When was that?' The fellow had clearly never heard of the project. He was looking at James as if he was Lazarus come out of the tomb.

'No matter. Good evening!' James said curtly, and he walked away. Then, although he had never before in his life succumbed to the temptation of talking to himself, now, because it was so important, he put himself a question out loud.

'Have I lost touch with Dublin?' he asked. And he had to answer simply and honestly. 'I have.' He should have known the library was always closed this month. If only there was a friend on whom he could call. But he'd lost touch with his friends too.

He looked around. There used to be a few eating places in this vicinity, or rather he could have sworn there were. It hardly seemed possible they were *all* closed down. Where on earth did people eat in Dublin nowadays? They surely didn't go to the hotels? In his day the small hotels were always given over at night to political rallies or football clubs. And the big hotels were out of the question. Not that he'd look into the cost at this stage. He stopped. If it was anywhere near time for his bus he wouldn't think twice of going straight back without eating at all.

It was all very well for Myra. She ate hardly anything anyway. He often felt that as far as food went, their meal together meant nothing to her. Setting up that damned unsteady card-table, and laying out those silly plates of hers shaped like vine leaves and too small to hold enough for a bird. They reminded him of when his sisters used to make him play babby-house.

Passing Trinity College, James saw there was still two hours to go before his bus, but it was just on the hour. There might be a bus going to Cavan? The Cavan bus passed through Garlow Cross, only a few miles from the cottage. How about taking that? He'd taken it once years ago, and although he was younger and fitter in those days, he was tempted to do it. His stomach was so empty it was almost caving in, but he doubted if he could eat anything now. He felt sickish. He might feel better after sitting in the bus. And better anything than hanging about the city.

At that moment on Aston Quay James saw the Cavan bus. It was filling up with passengers, and the conductor and driver, leaning on the parapet of the Liffey, were taking a last smoke. James was about to dash across the street, but first he dashed into a sweet shop to buy a bar of chocolate, or an apple. The sensation in his insides was like something gnawing at his guts. He got an apple and a bar of chocolate as well, but he nearly missed the bus. Very nearly. The driver was at the wheel and the engine was running. James had to put on a sprint to get across the street, and even then the driver was pulling on the big steering wheel and swivelling the huge wheels outward into the traffic before putting the bus in motion. James jumped on the step.

'Dangerous that, sir,' said the young conductor.

'You hadn't begun to move!' James replied testily, while he stood on the platform getting his breath back.

'Could have jerked forward, sir. Just as you were stepping up!'

'You think a toss would finish me off, eh?' James

said. He meant the words to be ironical, but his voice hadn't been lighthearted enough to carry off the joke.

The conductor didn't smile. 'Never does any of us any good, sir, at any age.'

James looked at him with hatred. The fellow was thin and spectacled. Probably the over-conscientious sort. Feeling no inclination to make small talk he lurched into the body of the bus, and sat down on the nearest seat. He was certainly glad to be off his feet. He hadn't noticed until now how they ached. Such a day. Little did he think setting off that it would be a case of About Turn and Quick March.

James slumped down in his seat, but when he felt the bulge of the apple in his pocket he brightened up, and was about to take it out when he was overcome by a curious awkwardness with regard to the conductor. Instead, keeping his hand buried in his pocket he broke off a piece of the chocolate and surreptitiously put it into his mouth. He would nearly have been too tired to chew the apple. He settled back on the seat and tried to doze. But now Myra's words kept coming back. They were repeating on him, like indigestion.

To think she should taunt him with how long they'd known each other? Wasn't it a good thing they'd been able to put up with each other for so long? What else but time had cemented their relationship? As she herself had once put it, very aptly, they'd invested a lot in each other. Well, as far as he was concerned she could have counted on *her* investment to the end. Wasn't it their credo that it didn't take marriage lines to bind together people of their integrity. He had not told her, not in so many words – from delicacy – but he had made provision for her in his will. He'd been rather proud of the way he'd worded the bequest too, putting in a few lines of appreciation that were, he thought, gracefully, but more important, tactfully expressed.

Oh, why had she doubted him? Few wives could be as sure of their husbands as she of him – but he had to amend this – as she *ought* to be, because clearly she had set no value on his loyalty. What was that she'd said about the deprivations she'd suffered? *'One of the many deprivations!'* Those might not have been her exact words, but that was more or less what she'd implied. What had come over her? He shook his head. Had they not agreed that theirs was the perfect solution for facing into the drearier years of ageing and decay? That dreary time was not imminent, of course, but alas it would inevitably come. The process of ageing was not attractive, and they both agreed that if they were continually together – well, really married for instance – the afflictions of age would be doubled for them. On the other hand, with the system they'd worked out, neither saw anything but what was best, and best preserved, in the other. As the grosser aspects of age became discernible, if they could not conceal them from themselves, at least they could conceal them from each other. To put it flatly, if they had been married a dozen times over, that would still be the way he'd want things to be at the end. It was disillusioning now to find she had not seen eye to eye with him on this. Worse still, she'd gone along with him and paid lip-service to his ideals while underneath she must all the time have dissented.

Suddenly James sat bolt upright. That word she used: deprivation. She couldn't have meant that he'd done her out of children? What a thought! Surely it was unlikely that she could have had a child even when they first met? What age was she then? Well, perhaps not too old but surely to God she was at an age when she couldn't have fancied putting herself in *that* condition? And what about all the cautions that were given now on the danger of late conception? How would *she* like to be saddled with a retarded child? Why, it was her who first told him about recent medical findings! And – wait a minute – that was early in their acquaintance too, if he remembered rightly. He could recall certain particulars of the conversation. They had been discussing her work, and the demands it made on her. She was, of course, aware from the first that *he* never wanted children, that he abhorred the thought of a houseful of brats, crawling everywhere, and dribbling and spitting out food. They overran a place. As for the smell of wet diapers about a house, it nauseated him. She'd pulled him up on that though.

'Not soiled diapers, James. The most slovenly woman in the world has more self-respect than to leave dirty diapers lying about. But I grant you there often is a certain odour – I've found it myself at times in the homes of my friends, and it has surprised me, I must say – but it comes from *clean* diapers hanging about to air. At worst it's the smell of steam. They have to be boiled you know.' She made a face. 'I agree with you, though. It's not my favourite brand of perfume.'

Those were her very words. If he were to be put in the dock at this moment he could swear to it. Did that sound like a woman who wanted a family? Yet tonight she had insinuated – James was so furious he clenched his hands and dug his feet into the floor-

o

boards as if the bus were about to hurtle over the edge of an abyss and he could put a brake on it.

Then he thought of something else: something his sister Kay had said.

It was the time Myra had had to go into hospital for a few weeks. Nothing serious, she'd said. Nothing to worry about, or so she'd told him. Just a routine tidying up job that most people – presumably she meant women – thought advisable. Naturally he'd encouraged her to get it over and done with: not to put it on the long finger. The shocking thing was how badly it had shaken her. He was appalled at how frightful she'd looked for months afterwards. Finally the doctors ordered her to take a good holiday, although it hadn't been long since her summer holidays. She hadn't gone away that summer, except for one long week-end in London, but she'd packed up her work and he'd gone up more often. But the doctor was insistent that this time she was to go away. Oddly enough, her going away had hit him harder than her going into hospital. If they could have gone away together it would have been different. That, of course, was impossible. There was no longer a spot on the globe where one mightn't run the risk of bumping into some busybody from Dublin.

'What will I do while you're away?' he'd asked.

'Why don't you come up here as usual,' she suggested, 'except you need order only one tray.'

But she over-estimated the charm of the flat for its own sake. And he told her so.

'Nonsense,' she said. 'Men are like cats and dogs; it's their habitat they value, not the occupants.'

'I'll tell you what I'll do,' he said finally. 'I'll come up the day you're coming back and I'll have a fire lit – how about that?'

'Oh James, you are a dear. It would make me so glad to be coming back.'

'I should hope you'd be glad to be coming back anyway?'

'Oh yes, but you must admit it would be extra special to be coming back to find you here – in our little nest.'

There! James slapped his knee. *That* was where he'd got the word nest. He had to hand it to her; she was very ingenious in avoiding the word 'home'. She was at her best when it came to these small subtleties other people overlooked. And the day she was due back he had fully intended to be in the flat before her, were it not for a chance encounter with his sister Kay and a remark of hers that upset him.

Kay knew all about Myra. Whether she approved of her or not James did not know: Kay and himself were too much alike to embarrass each other by confidences. That was why he found what she said that day so extraordinary.

'Very sensible of her to go away,' Kay had said, 'otherwise it takes a long time, I believe, to recover from that beastly business.' Beastly business? What did she mean? Unlike herself, Kay had gone on and on. 'Much messier than childbirth I understand. Also, I've heard, James, that it's worse for an unmarried woman – ' she paused – 'I mean a childless woman.' Then feeling – as well she might – that she'd overstepped herself, she looked at her watch. 'I'll have to fly,' she said. And perhaps to try and excuse her indiscretion she resorted to something else that was rare for Kay – banality. 'It's sort of the end of the road for them, I suppose,' she said, before she hurried away leaving him confused and dismayed.

He had never bothered to ask Myra what her operation had been. He didn't see that it concerned him. At any age there were certain danger zones for a woman that had to be kept under observation. But what if it had been a hysterectomy! Was that any business of his? Medically speaking, it wasn't all that different from any other ectomy – tonsillectomy, appendectomy. What was so beastly about it? If it came to that, the most frightful mess of all was getting one's antrums cleaned out. He knew all about *that*. Anyway the whole business was outside his province. Or at least he had thought so then.

Then, then, then. But now, now it was as if he'd been asked to stand up and testify to something. It was most unfair. Myra herself had never arraigned him. Neither before nor after. Admittedly he had not given her much encouragement. But he could have sworn that she herself hadn't given a damn at the time. Ah, but – and this was the rub, the whole business could have bred resentment, could have rankled within her and gone foetid. Considered in this new light the taunts she had flung at him tonight could no longer be put down to hysteria and written off – something long festering had suppurated. He put his hand to his head. Dear God, to think she had allowed him to bask all those years in a fool's paradise!

He closed his eyes. Thank heavens he hadn't demeaned himself by going back to try and patch things up. He'd left the way open should he decide to sever the bond completely. Perhaps he ought to sever it, if only on the principle that if a person once tells you a lie, that puts an end to truth between you forever. A lie always made him feel positively sick. And God knows he felt sick enough as it was. There was a definite burning sensation now in his chest as well as his stomach. He looked around the steamy bus. Could it be the fumes of the engine that were affecting him? He'd have liked to go and stand on the platform to get some fresh air, but he hated to make himself notice-able, although the bus was now nearly empty. He stole a look at the other passengers to see if anyone was watching him. He might have been muttering to him-self, or making peculiar faces. Just to see if anyone would notice he stealthily, but deliberately, made a face into the window, on which the steam acted like a backing of mercury. And sure enough the damn con-ductor was looking straight at him. James felt he had to give the fellow a propitiating grin, which the im-pudent fellow took advantage of immediately.

'Not yet, sir,' he said. 'I'll tell you when you're there!'

Officious again. Well, smart as he was, he didn't know his countryside. Clearing a space on the foggy glass, James looked out. It was getting dark outside now but the shape of the trees could still be seen against the last light in the west. The conductor was wrong! They *were* there!' He jumped to his feet.

'Not yet, sir,' the blasted fellow called out again, and loudly this time for all to hear.

Ignoring him, James staggered down the bus to the boarding-platform, where, without waiting for the conductor to do it, he defiantly hit the bell to bring the bus to a stop. The fellow merely shrugged his shoulders. James threw an angry glance at him, and then, although the bus had not quite stopped, deliberately and only taking care to face the way the bus was travelling so that if he did fall it would be less dangerous, he jumped off.

Luckily he did not fall. He felt a bit shaken, as he regained his balance precariously on the dark road, he was glad to think he had spiked that conductor. He could tell he had by the smart way the fellow hit the bell again and set the bus once more in motion, that for all his solicitude on the Quays, he'd hardly have noticed if one had fallen on one's face on the road: or cared.

And Myra? If Myra were to read a report of the accident in the newspaper tomorrow, how would *she* feel? More interesting still – what would she tell her friends? Secretive as their relationship was supposed to be, James couldn't help wondering if she might not have let the truth leak out to some people. Indeed, this suspicion had lurked in his mind for some time, but he only fully faced it now.

What about those phone calls she sometimes got? Those times when she felt it necessary to plug out the phone and carry it into her bedroom? Or else talk in a lowered voice, very different from the normal way in which she'd call out 'wrong number' and bang down the receiver? Now that he thought about it, the worst give-away was when she'd let the phone ring and ring without answering it at all. It nearly drove him mad listening to that ringing.

'What will they think, Myra?' he'd cry. When she used to say the caller would think she was out, he nearly went demented altogether at her lack of logic.

'They wouldn't keep on ringing if they didn't suspect you were here,' he exploded once.

Ah! The insidiousness of her answer hadn't fully registered at the time. *Now* it did though.

'Oh, they'll understand.' That was what she'd said.

Understand what? He could only suppose she had given her friends some garbled explanation of things.

'Oh damn her! Damn her!' he said out loud again. There was no reason now why he shouldn't talk out loud or shout if he liked here on the lonely country road. 'Damn, damn,' he shouted. 'Damn, damn, damn!'

Immediately James felt uncomfortable. What if there was someone listening? A few yards ahead, to the left, there was a lighted window. But suddenly he was alerted to something odd. There should not be a light on the left. The shop at the crossroads should be on the other side. He looked around. Could that rotten little conductor have been right? Had he got off too soon? Perhaps that was why the fellow had hit that bell so smartly? To give him no time to discover his mistake?

For clearly he *had* made a mistake, and a bloody great one. He peered into the darkness. But the night was too black, he could see nothing. He had no choice but to walk on.

By the time James had passed the cottage with the lighted window, his eyes were getting more used to the dark. All the same when a rick of hay reared up to one side of the road it might have been a mountain! Where was he at all? And a few seconds later when unexpectedly the moon slipped out from behind the clouds and glinted on the tin roof of a shed in the distance it might have been the sheen of a lake for all he recognised of his whereabouts. Just then, however, he caught sight of the red tail light of the bus again. It had only disappeared because the bus had dipped into a valley. It was now climbing out of the dip again, and going up a steep hill. Ah! he knew that hill. He wasn't as far off his track as he thought. Only a quarter of a mile or so, but he shook his head. In his present state that was about enough to finish him. Still, things could have been worse.

Meanwhile a wisp of vapoury cloud had come between the moon and the earth and in a few minutes it was followed by a great black bank of cloud. Only for a thin green streak in the west it would have been pitch dark again. This streak shed no light on his way but it acted on James like a sign, an omen.

He passed the hayrick. He passed the tin shed. But now another mass of blackness rose up to the left and came between him and the sky. It even hid the green streak this time though he was able to tell by a sudden resinous scent in the air and a curious warmth that the road was passing through a small wood. His spirits rose at once. These were the trees he could see from his cottage. Immediately, his mistake less disastrous, the distance lessened. If only that conductor could know how quickly he had got his bearings! The impudent fellow probably thought he'd left him properly stranded. And perhaps as much to spite the impudent fellow as anything else, when at that instant a daring thought entered his mind and he gave it heed. What if he were to cut diagonally across this wood? It could save him half a mile. It would actually be putting his mistake to work for him.

'What about it, James? Come on. Be a sport,' he jovially exhorted himself.

And seeing that his green banner was again faintly discernible through the dark trees, he called on it to be his lodestar, and scrambled up on the grass bank that separated the road from the wood.

James was in the wood before it came home to him that of course this must be Asigh wood – it must belong to the Balfes! No matter. Why should he let that bother him? The wood was nowhere near their house as far as he remembered its position by daylight. It was composed mostly of neglected, self-seeded trees, more scrub than timber – almost waste ground – ground that had probably deteriorated into commonage.

As he advanced into the little copse – wood was too grand a designation for it – James saw it was not as dense as it seemed from the road, or else at this point there was a pathway through it. Probably it was a short cut well known to the locals, because even in the dark, he thought he saw sodden cigarette packets on the ground, and there were toffee wrappers and orange peels lodged in the bushes. Good signs.

Further in, however, his path was unexpectedly blocked by a fallen tree. It must have been a long time lying on the ground because when he put his hand on it to climb over, it was wet and slimy. He quickly withdrew his hand in disgust. He'd have to make his way round it.

The path was not very well defined on the other side of the log. It looked as if people did not after all penetrate this far. The litter at the edge of the wood had probably been left by children. Or by lovers who only wanted to get out of sight of the road? Deeper in, the scrub was thicker, and in one place he mistook a strand of briar for barbed wire it was so tough and hard to cut through. You'd need wire clippers!

James stopped. Was it foolhardy to go on? He'd already ripped the sleeve of his suit. However the pain in his stomach gave him his answer. Nothing that would get him home quicker was foolish.

'Onward, James,' he said wearily.

And then, damn it, he came to another fallen tree. Again he had to work his way around it. Mind you, he hadn't counted on this kind of thing. The upper branches of this tree spread out over an incredibly wide area. From having to look down, instead of up, he found that – momentarily of course – he'd lost his sense of direction. Fortunately, through the trees, he could take direction from his green banner. Fixing on it, he forged ahead.

But now there were new hazards. At least twice, tree stumps nearly tripped him, and there were now dried ruts that must have been made by timber lorries at some distant date. Lucky he didn't sprain his ankle. He took out his handkerchief and wiped his forehead. At this rate he wouldn't make very quick progress. He was beginning to ache in every limb, and when he drew a breath, a sharp pain ran through him. The pains in his stomach were indistinguishable now from all the other pains in his body. It was like the way a tooth-ache could turn the whole of one's face into one great ache. The thought of turning back plagued him too at every step. Stubbornly, though, he resisted the thought of turning. To go on could hardly be much worse than to go back through those briars?

A second later James got a fall, a nasty fall. Without

warning, a crater opened up in front of him and he went head-first into it. Another fallen tree, blown over in a storm evidently, because the great root that had been ripped out of the ground had taken clay and all with it, leaving this gaping black hole. Oh God! He picked himself up and mopped his forehead with his sleeves.

This time he had to make a wide detour. Luckily after that the wood seemed to be thinning out. He was able to walk a bit faster, and so it seemed reasonable to deduce that he might be getting near to the road at the other end. His relief was so great that perhaps that was why he did not pause to take his bearings again, and when he did look up he was shocked to see the green streak in the sky was gone. Or was it? He swung around. No, it was there, but it seemed to have veered around and was now behind him. Did that mean he was going in the wrong direction? Appalled, he leant back against a tree. His legs were giving way under him. He would not be able to go another step without a rest. And now a new pain had struck him between the the shoulders. He felt around with his foot in the darkness looking for somewhere to sit, but all he could feel were wads of soggy leaves from summers dead and gone.

Perhaps it was just as well – if he sat down he might not be able to get up again. Then the matter was taken out of his hands. He was attacked by a fit of dizziness, and his head began to reel. To save himself from falling he dropped down on one knee and braced himself with the palms of his hands against the ground. Bad as he was, the irony of his posture struck him – the sprinter, tensed for the starter's pistol! Afraid of cramp he cautiously got to his feet. And he thought of the times when, as a youngster playing hide and seek, a rag would be tied over his eyes and he would be spun around like a top, so that when the blindfold was removed, he wouldn't know which way to run.

Ah, there was the green light! But how it had narrowed! It was only a thin line now. Still, James lurched towards it. The bushes had got dense again and he was throwing himself against them, as against a crashing wave, while they for their part seemed to thrust him back. Coming to a really thick clump he gathered up enough strength to hurl himself against it, only to find that he went through it as if it was a bank of fog, and sprawled out into another clearing.

Was it the road at last? No. It would have been lighter overhead. Instead a solid mass of blackness towered over him, high as the sky. Were it not for his lifeline of light he would have despaired. As if it too might quench he feverishly fastened his eyes on it. It was not a single line any more. There were three or four lines. Oh God, no? It was a window, a window with a green blind drawn down, that let out only the outline of its light. A house? Oh God, not Balfe's? In absolute panic James turned and with the vigour of frenzy crashed back through the undergrowth in the way he had come. This time the bushes gave way freely before him, but the silence that had pressed so dank upon him was shattered at every step and he was betrayed by the snapping and breaking of twigs. When a briar caught on his sleeve it gave out a deafening rasp. Pricks from a gorse bush bit into his flesh like sparks of fire, but worse still was the prickly heat of shame that ran over his whole body.

'Damn, damn, damn,' he cried, not caring suddenly what noise he made. Why had he run like that? – Like a madman? – Using up his last store of strength? What did he care about anyone or anything if only he could get out of this place? What if it was Balfe's? It was hardly the house? Probably an outbuilding? Or the quarters of a hired hand? Why hadn't he called out?

Sweat was breaking out all over him now and he had to exert a superhuman strength not to let himself fall spent, on the ground, because if he did he'd stay there. He wouldn't be able to get up. To rest for a minute he dropped on one knee again. The pose of the athlete again! Oh, it was a pity Myra couldn't see him, he thought bitterly, but then for a moment he had a crazy feeling that the pose was for real. He found himself tensing the muscles of his face, as if at any minute a real shot would blast-off and he would spring up and dash madly down a grassy sprint-track.

It was then that a new, a terrible, an utterly un-endurable pain exploded in his chest.

'God, God!' he cried. His hands under him were riveted to the ground. Had he been standing he would have been thrown. 'What is the matter with me?' he cried. And the question rang out over all the wood. Then, as another spasm went through him other questions were torn from him. Was it a heart attack? A stroke? – In abject terror, not daring to stir, he stayed crouched. 'Ah, Ah, Ahh . . . ' The pain again. The pain, the pain, the pain.

'Am I dying?' he gasped, but this time it was the pain that answered, and answered so strangely James didn't understand, because it did what he did not think possible: it catapulted him to his feet, and filled him with a strength that never, never in his life had he possessed. It ran through him like a bar of iron – a stanchion that held his ribs together. He was turned into a man of iron! If he raised his arms now and thrashed about, whole trees would give way before him, and their branches, brittle as glass, would clatter to the ground. 'See Myra! See!' he cried out. So he had lost his vigour? He'd show her! But he had taken his eyes off the light. Where was it? Had it gone out? 'I told you not to go out,' he yelled at it, and lifting his iron feet he went crashing towards where he had seen it last.

But the next minute he knew there was something wrong. Against his face he felt something wet and cold, and he was almost overpowered by the smell of rank earth and rotting leaves. If he'd fallen he hadn't felt the fall. Was he numbed? He raised his head. He'd have to get help. But when he tried to cry out no sound came.

The light? Where was it. 'Oh, don't go out,' he pleaded to it, as if it was the light of life itself, and to propitiate it, he gave it a name. 'Don't go out, Emmy,' he prayed. Then came the last and most anguished question of all. Was he raving? No, no. It was only a window. But in his head there seemed to be a dialogue of two voices, his own and another that answered derisively 'What window?' James tried to explain that it was the window in the classroom. Hadn't he opened it when the big footballer wasn't able to pull down the sash? He, James, had leant across the desk and brought it down with one strong pull. But where was the rush of sweet summer air? There was only a deathly chill. And where was Emmy?

With a last desperate effort James tried to stop his mind from stumbling and tried to fasten it on Myra. Where was *she*? She wouldn't have failed him. But she *had* failed him. Both of them had failed him. Under a weight of bitterness too great to be borne his face was pressed into the wet leaves, and when he gulped for breath, the rotted leaves were sucked into his mouth.